"This case is getting too dangerous— I want you to drive out of here, get back to Chicago as quickly as you can."

If he hadn't said it so softly, hadn't looked at her as if she were his top priority, maybe she wouldn't have had that deep ache tear through her chest. "No way. I'm not going anywhere. If I go back, you win."

He said nothing, just stared at her lips as if he didn't understand the words she had uttered.

"Stop."

His gaze rose to hers. He blinked. "What?"

"Stop staring at my mouth."

He swallowed visibly. "I...was thinking."

Yeah, so was she. Usually that was a good thing, but in this case it was a problem.

"This is ridiculous." She grabbed him by the shoulders, went up on tiptoe and kissed him firmly on the mouth.

His arms suddenly went around her waist, pulled her against him. He kissed her hard...long...deeply.

The kiss was worth every moment of frustration and irritation and waiting.

DEBRA WEBB

COLBY CONTROL

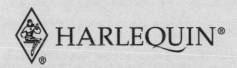

TORONTO • NEW YORK • LONDON
AMSTERDAM • PARIS • SYDNEY • HAMBURG
STOCKHOLM • ATHENS • TOKYO • MILAN • MADRID
PRAGUE • WARSAW • BUDAPEST • AUCKLAND

This book is dedicated to my lovely niece, Tanya.
Her many visits to Las Vegas inspired me
to set this story in that unique city.
Tanya is very much like my character Nora Friedman—
she is determined to succeed
no matter the trials that befall her.

ISBN-13: 978-0-373-74537-1

COLBY CONTROL

Recycling programs
for this product may
not exist in your area.

Copyright © 2010 by Debra Webb

www.eHarlequin.com

Printed in U.S.A.

ABOUT THE AUTHOR

Debra Webb wrote her first story at age nine and her first romance at thirteen. It wasn't until she spent three years working for the military behind the Iron Curtain and within the confining political walls of Berlin, Germany, that she realized her true calling. A five-year stint with NASA on the space shuttle program reinforced her love of the endless possibilities within her grasp as a storyteller. A collision course between suspense and romance was set. Debra has been writing romantic suspense and action packed romantic thrillers since. Visit her at www.DebraWebb.com or write to her at P.O. Box 4889, Huntsville, AL 35815.

Books by Debra Webb

CAST OF CHARACTERS

Ted Tallant—Ted is not looking forward to working his first case with former Equalizer Nora Friedman. There is something about the woman that drives him crazy... but will she hold up her end of the partnership when teamwork means the difference between life and death?

Nora Friedman—Nora is fine with the merger between the Equalizers and the Colby Agency...as long as she never, ever has to work with Ted Tallant.

Heather Vandiver—She is certain the cousin she hasn't seen in decades, Victoria Colby-Camp, can save her.

Dr. Brent Vandiver—Renowned cosmetic surgeon Brent Vandiver has it all...but there is only one thing he really wants. Who has to die to ensure his happiness?

Camille Soto—Camille moved up the ranks in the glitzy casino world in record time. Perhaps it's her time between the sheets that makes her so popular.

Ivan Romero—Ivan professes to own Sin City. No one dares to cross him. Nora Friedman made that mistake once. Now she's back in his city and he intends to make her pay.

Victoria Colby-Camp—As the head of the Colby Agency, Victoria is committed to making the merger between her agency and the Equalizers work.

Jim Colby—Jim wants his mother to be happy, no matter what it takes. All he has to do is keep his team in line during this awkward transition.

Simon Ruhl—As Victoria's second-in-command, Simon works hard to keep the peace between the Colby Agency staff and the newcomers.

Leland Rockford (Rocky)—Another of the former Equalizers. Rocky is tasked with protecting Heather Vandiver.

Chapter One

Inside the Colby Agency
Monday, 9:05 a.m.

Ted Tallant waited in Victoria Colby-Camp's office as requested. This morning's briefing had been a little wild and a lot freaky. The merger talks between the agency and the Equalizers had been going on for months. Contracts and benefits and legal technicalities had been resolved. A number of orientation and training sessions had been conducted between those in charge here at the Colby Agency and the staff members of the former Equalizers.

The deal was done and all involved would have to get used to the changes.

Today the four from the Equalizers shop who had opted to make the transition had been officially introduced as new agency staff members. Ben Steele, Leland Rockford, Evonne Cassidy and the infamous Nora Friedman.

Irritation tightened Ted's jaw even as her name filtered through his brain. *Nora.* The woman was a looker; he couldn't deny that. Tall and willowy, with sleek black hair and dark, dark eyes. Her presence in a room set him on edge.

She specialized in deception.

Ted rolled his eyes. Yeah. *Deception.* The whole idea rankled the hell out of him. But it was an Equalizer thing. Jim Colby, Victoria's son, had started the Equalizers five years ago, and he'd made it a point to hire the very best at going around and through the law.

Five months had passed since Victoria and her son had made the decision to move forward with the merger. Tension had been running high since. Nothing about the plan had been easy. Jim had acquiesced to Victoria's operating rules and code of conduct for the most part, but keeping the members of his former staff in line had proven a pain in the butt.

Not that a single one of his former Equalizer team was anything other than highly skilled and admittedly brilliant. But they had their way of doing things and change wasn't coming easy.

What ticked Ted off the most about Nora was the fact that she not only understood she was brilliant, but she also reveled in the idea.

Ted was just a regular guy. Born and raised in the heartland of Idaho. He'd spent a few years working as a skip tracer back home. After earning a criminal justice degree at Boise State University, he'd quickly learned that law enforcement—at least as a cop—wasn't for him. Too much red tape, too often the victims were the victims on both sides of the law. So he'd committed to freelancing for a couple of P.I. firms.

Six years of experience had landed him

an opportunity with the Colby Agency— the very best in the business of private investigations.

And Nora Friedman wasn't going to make him miserable no matter if she questioned or challenged every word he said. She had, apparently, selected him to be her verbal punching bag. Maybe she was still frustrated with the change in rules dictated by the merger. After all, following rules, period, didn't appear to be her preferred professional model.

The door behind him opened and Ted kicked Nora Friedman right out of his head. He stood and turned to greet his boss as she strode into the room. "Morning, Victoria."

"Good morning, Ted." She beamed a smile that only Victoria Colby-Camp could produce. The woman was amazing. Nothing stopped her. And the bad guys tried. Oh, did they try. January's siege was a prime example of just how unstoppable the lady had proved time and time again. One of the aspects of working at this agency that pleased Ted the most was a boss who never expected anything out of her investigators she wasn't prepared to do herself.

When she'd rounded her desk, her gaze locked with his. "I'm sorry to keep you waiting, Ted." Victoria gestured to the chair he'd vacated. "Let's sit. This may take some time."

"Yes, ma'am." Ted dropped back into his seat while Victoria settled into the big, lush leather one behind her desk. Sounded like he had a new assignment. He would be only too happy to get away from the office while the dust settled on the merger. Nora Know-It-All Friedman was making him crazy.

The boss took a moment to organize what appeared to be notes she'd made. When she turned her attention back to him, he didn't miss the worry in her eyes. "I had a very disturbing call this morning, immediately following the weekly briefing."

Ted wasn't really surprised to hear that. Since the siege back in January and the subsequent steps the agency had been forced to take, there had been a series of disturbing events. The powers that be at the Colby Agency, Victoria, Jim, Ian Michaels and Simon Ruhl, had been working overtime to sort out legal details and to smooth ruffled feathers. With the help of Victoria's husband, Lucas Camp, most of the trouble, legally speaking, was behind them at this point. But there remained a considerable ways to go in getting all phases of the numerous changes reconciled.

Thankfully the media frenzy had calmed. The trials against former district attorney Timothy Gordon and crime lord Reginald Clark were under way. Leonard Thorp, the stepfather of one of Clark's victims, was extremely ill and very near death. He'd already outlived the few months he'd been given when diagnosed with terminal cancer. His devoted wife, who kept the agency posted on his condition, claimed the oncologist treating her husband insisted the man simply didn't want to die. Most of the folks here at the Colby Agency figured he had no intention of dying until he saw that Reginald Clark was sentenced to a proper punishment for his vicious crimes.

Thorp, due to his illness, had been sentenced to house arrest for orchestrating the siege against the Colby Agency. No one, including the new Cook County D.A., wanted to see the man go to prison when he would certainly be dead before his three attorneys finished their stall tactics. An acceptable plea bargain had settled the issue. Particularly since Thorp's hired gun, Pederson, had been the one behind the two fatalities. Pederson had taken it upon himself to cross that line. For all his extreme measures, Thorp hadn't actually wanted anyone to die—except Reginald Clark.

Then the merger between the Equalizers and the Colby Agency had commenced. To Ted's way of thinking, the presence of Nora and her colleagues was almost another siege in and of itself. But Ted kept his mouth shut and hoped it would all work out…eventually.

"A call?" Ted repeated when Victoria remained seemingly lost in thought.

She gave her head a visible shake. "I'm sorry. I…" Victoria drew in a deep breath. "I was so surprised when I received the call. I'm still a little stunned."

After all Victoria had been through the past year, Ted had to wonder what could shock her as much as this call clearly had.

"I have a distant cousin—by marriage—in Los Angeles." She paused, her expression reflecting the faraway path her thoughts had taken. "I haven't heard from her in years…decades actually."

"There's a problem," said Ted, guessing. Whatever the situation, Victoria was genuinely shaken.

"Yes." She nodded, the movement hesitant, thoughtful. "She's only thirty-eight. My mother's younger sister was her stepmother. But my entire family died out years ago. Heather…" Victoria looked directly at Ted. "Her name is Heather. She never clicked with her stepmother, my aunt. In fact, it's safe to say Heather wanted nothing to do with any of our family…until now."

That was relatives for you. Win the lottery or let someone you haven't heard from in decades have a problem and suddenly you're *family* again.

"Her husband is a cosmetic surgeon and she believes he is cheating on her."

Ted wanted to feel sorry for the woman but the only person he really felt sorry for at the moment was Victoria. Her pained expression told just how deeply the situation had affected her. "Does she have reason to believe he's done this before?"

Victoria considered the question a moment. "Heather is certain this is nothing new. She says she can prove a pattern over the past several years. But this time is different." Again Victoria's gaze met his. And this time the pain had turned to worry. "Heather believes her husband wants her out of the way…*permanently.*"

"And California is a community property state," Ted observed. He got the whole picture now. A divorce would mean the husband would have to share. A sudden, accidental death would leave him everything—including any death benefits from life insurance policies.

"Her brakes went out in her car," Victoria went on. "*Her one-hundred-ten-thousand-dollar car.* The crash was minor only because of her quick thinking and sheer luck. She's terrified to leave the house now."

"Did a certified mechanic find evidence of foul play?" Brakes occasionally went out...even on the high-end vehicles. Usually a faulty part or system. It wasn't unheard-of and happened to the best of automobiles. But he didn't have to tell his boss that.

Victoria shrugged. "Her husband insisted on seeing to the repairs, so Heather can't say for an absolute certainty."

"Could be paranoia," Ted suggested simply because it was a plausible possibility. He didn't know this Heather but he did know Victoria. If she thought the situation merited looking into, there had to be more than the brake failure incident.

"She awakened to a gas leak just last week. Her husband had already left for work." Victoria sent Ted a pointed look. "I suppose it's possible their five-star gas range had some defective part, as well."

He agreed. A second *accident* in such a short time frame was a little too neat for a mere coincidence. "I see your point."

"Her husband also has a practice in Vegas," Victoria explained. "He spends one week each month there. The woman he is allegedly seeing on the side lives there. She's a manager at one of the casinos. According to Heather, her husband is in Vegas this week. She wants to find out what he and his mistress are planning, particularly if it involves her continued well-being—or lack thereof."

"What about protection for your cousin?" Ted didn't have to point out to Victoria that being out of town when his wife got murdered during a robbery attempt at the house was a useful alibi. Ted felt confident she had already considered that scenario.

"I'm sending Leland Rockford to L.A. to keep an eye on Heather," she said, confirming his speculation, "but I'd very much like you to look into the husband's activities. Your background in finding people and information will be immensely useful."

Ted had never been to Vegas. It would be hotter than blazes this time of year, but the assignment sounded intriguing personally as well as professionally. This was his specialty. "Absolutely. I can leave immediately."

"Good. Mildred is working on travel arrangements now." Victoria cleared her throat, glanced around her desktop, avoiding eye contact. "As you know, we're working to integrate Jim's team with ours, and the best way to do that is to share assignments. Let those folks see how we do things firsthand."

Ted had known that was coming. Victoria didn't need to be worried about his cooperation. "Not a problem. I'll work in conjunction with Rocky. Keep him up to speed so that the wife knows what's going on at all times." Leland Rockford, Rocky, was a cool guy. A team player. Ted was immensely grateful that he would be working with Rocky and not that uptight, snobby...

"I'm glad you feel that way," Victoria replied, cutting into his assessment. "Jim is briefing Nora now. I'm certain the two of you will make a great team."

"Nora?" He couldn't have heard that right. "I thought you were talking about Rocky." About forty pounds of concrete settled in Ted's gut.

"I'm aware," said Victoria, broaching the subject gingerly, "that you and Nora don't see eye to eye on many things. But Nora has experience in the Vegas casino world. She knows her way around that setting. Her knowledge will be an invaluable asset."

Ted felt sick. "As long as *she* is aware that I'm lead in this investigation," he said, hoping like hell that would be the case.

"Of course," Victoria assured him. "You will be lead. No question. Nora's job is to watch and learn. She's a skilled investigator, but it's very important that Jim's staff becomes acquainted with the way we do things here at the Colby Agency. My goal is to see that each of the Equalizers who opted to come on board works with each member of the agency. An acquaintance rotation of sorts. I feel that strategy will create a deeper sense of cohesion more quickly."

He couldn't fault her approach. "I'm certain her knowledge of the casino world will be useful." The words were bitter in his mouth. Ted wanted to bite off his tongue at the reality of what his agreement meant.

He would be spending every minute of every hour for the next few days in a city he'd never visited with Nora the know-it-all, who evidently knew her way around the place. Perfect.

"I'm counting on you, Ted," Victoria said, again interrupting his troubling tirade. "This merger is of the utmost importance to me. I want every aspect of the transition to go as smoothly as possible."

What could he say? Ted loved working at the Colby Agency. He respected and admired Victoria. He couldn't possibly let her down.

"Yes, ma'am," he promised. "You can definitely count on me. I'll get the job done and show Nora the ropes."

If he didn't kill her first.

Chapter Two

"You are kidding?" This couldn't be possible. Nora shuddered at the idea of working with Tallant. No way, no how. His mere presence in a room grated on her nerves like no one else she'd ever met.

He made her...*uneasy.*

"This is the way we'll be doing things for a while," Jim Colby reminded her. "Until the transition is complete, we'll be working in pairs. Tallant will be lead. You'll watch and learn."

"Learn what?" Jim had to be out of his mind. There was no way on earth she could learn one thing from good old boy Ted Tallant. No way!

He was... He was too...*I'm in charge.*

"The Colby Agency has a certain way of doing things. There's more finesse involved. As a Colby investigator you will be playing by the rules." Jim narrowed his gaze for emphasis. "*All* the rules."

This was ludicrous! "I don't need anyone to teach me that," she snapped. "The guidelines for conducting an investigation have been laid out over and over. Does Victoria think we're stupid?"

Nora instantly regretted the remark. The shadow that passed over Jim's face warned that his patience was thinning. He'd almost lost his mother. He was going above and beyond to ensure he pleased her. Which ultimately made life damned frustrating for Nora and her comrades, the other former Equalizers. *Former* being the operative word here.

"Do we have a problem, Nora?" Jim's face cleared instantly, his expression wholly unreadable now. "Four months ago you were given an option of coming on board with the Colby Agency or six weeks' severance pay going out the door.

If you've changed your mind, now's the time to speak up."

Her bad choice of words had left a seriously bad taste. She'd stuck her foot, stiletto included, directly into her mouth this time. "No. I…" She heaved a disgusted breath. "*We* don't have a problem. I just don't like Ted, that's all."

"You don't have to like him," Jim offered. "You just have to follow his orders."

Well, that made all the difference in the world. "I can do whatever I have to do." Working for Jim had given her the credibility she'd been looking for her whole adult life. Joining the Colby Agency crew would add prestige to her position. She wasn't a fool. This was a priceless opportunity.

More than that…it offered her a way to continue helping those who needed it most. Generally when people came to a P.I. group, they were desperate because they hadn't been able to find that help with the police. Maybe here the clientele would be a little less desperate and a lot more inclined to want discretion, but according to Jim, there were still plenty who were truly desperate for the right and fair kind of help Nora liked to provide. What more could she ask for?

She wasn't letting a smart aleck like Ted Tallant screw this opportunity up for her. Working with him this one time wouldn't be the end of the world. All she had to do was look at it for what it was—a bad assignment in an otherwise good job.

"I'm good to go." She produced the expected smile. "You know I'll do whatever I have to in order to facilitate the merger."

"Good." Jim passed a file across his desk. "You'll find the details about the case there. Victoria is briefing Ted. It's imperative that the two of you get on location as quickly as possible. We have reason to believe time is not on our client's side. When we're done here, check with Mildred about the travel arrangements."

Nora couldn't wait. *Not.* She scanned the dossier on a Dr. Brent Vandiver, cosmetic surgeon. Forty-four. Judging by the photos, he'd been enjoying a number of the procedures he got the big bucks for performing on his patients. Store-bought tan and personal-trainer physique, all nicely packaged in a couture suit. Apparently the man had a penchant for infidelity.

Clearly this was a case that didn't include desperation in a real sense. Yeah.

"This isn't the first extramarital affair," Jim went on as she scanned the pages and photos, "but the wife feels that this time Vandiver wants his freedom with no strings attached."

Nora's gaze met Jim's. "He wants her out of the way, as in dead and gone."

Jim nodded. "She suspects so. I'm sending Rocky to L.A. to check out the wife. See if we're getting the whole story."

"I could do that and let Rocky work with Ted." Why the hell hadn't Jim laid it out that way in the first place? He had to know she couldn't stand Tallant. Why not make this easier for everyone? She'd gone to high school in L.A. Still had a mother there somewhere.

Probably still hawking her body downtown after business hours.

Jim's gaze narrowed once more. "Did you miss the part in the dossier that the mistress is a manager at a Vegas casino and hotel? Or that the husband is in Vegas as we speak?"

Damn. "I gotcha." Five years ago she'd completed an assignment in Vegas for her previous employer. Nora had spent eight weeks under deep cover there. She'd made it her business to know the ins and outs of the city...the life. Of course she was the logical candidate for the assignment.

Just her luck.

"We're square, right?" Jim stared at her with an unyielding gaze that warned he didn't want to hear otherwise. "This goes down just the way it's supposed to. No personal feelings getting in the way."

"Sure." She closed the file. Lifted her chin in defiance of the protests screaming in her head. "I'm a professional. Just because I'm better than Tallant doesn't mean I can't step back and learn—" she lifted one shoulder in a shrug "—*something* from him."

"You might just learn *something,* all right," Jim tossed back, his tone pointed.

Nora frowned at what was clearly a not-so-subtle reprimand. "I'm not sure I understand."

"When you stop learning," Jim explained, "that's when you no longer have a place in this business. No exceptions."

Enough said. "I understand." She stood. "Anything else?"

Jim moved his head from side to side. "Just remember, none of this changes what I expect from you, Nora. You're damned good. Don't let me down."

Nora's smile was real this time. "Now, that's one guarantee I can make without the first reservation. I will get the job done." For an Equalizer, failure was not an option. "I wouldn't dream of letting you down."

"Keep me posted," Jim said as he turned his attention to the mountain of files on his desk.

Jim Colby was in the process of reviewing every case the Colby Agency had worked for the past five years. His team, including Nora, was doing the same. The decision had been made, and he would do whatever it took to fit in...to make this merger work.

Nora would do the same.

All she had to do was get through this one assignment.

She exited his office and headed for Mildred Ballard's desk at the other end of the corridor. Her office was actually the small waiting area outside Victoria's office. Jim had taken an office at the opposite end of the corridor from his mother.

Space had been made for everyone.

As long as Nora had her space, she could deal with anything temporarily.

As she turned into Mildred's area, she came face-to-face with Tallant.

A truckload of frustration laced with a hint of disdain instantly drowned out her determination to play nice.

Maybe she was wrong...but she highly doubted an entire city block—or two—would be enough space between her and this guy.

The idea of spending the next few days with him, forced to submit to his lead… Well, maybe they would both survive.

One thing was certain, Nora would.

She had been equalizing situations long before she'd hired on with Jim Colby.

Tallant was the one who needed to be worried.

Chapter Three

Palomino Hotel and Casino, Las Vegas
4:00 p.m.

At least it wasn't the Copacabana.

Nora kicked aside the nasty memories that accompanied the thought. Five years was a long time. She hadn't heard a peep from the sick bastard in more than four of those years. Chances were she had nothing to worry about on that old score.

Still…she was back in Vegas.

There was always the possibility.

"That's her."

Nora blinked and followed Tallant's gaze. A tall, lithe blonde floated across the gaming floor, then paused to chat with a guest.

"Camille Soto," Tallant went on. "Twenty-eight. MBA from UCLA. She—"

"Yeah, yeah," said Nora, interrupting his narrative. "I read her dossier."

Tallant shot her a look.

Yeah, yeah. He was in charge. She was supposed to listen. Even if she already knew exactly what he was going to say.

"She was hired as an assistant manager for the casino one year ago. Promptly promoted to manager just six months ago."

Soto had grown up in Brentwood, a whole different world from Nora's North Hollywood roots. And Nora had barely finished high school, much less gotten a foot in the door of a fancy university.

"Our client's husband started…" Nora considered the best way to put it "He started interacting with Ms. Soto six months ago. Ironically about the same time she was promoted."

Tallant sipped his club soda as he watched the blonde schmooze with patrons.

"That's what the wife says, but we have no documented proof of the allegation."

Nora had a feeling there was more to this than she knew. Jim had gone over the file with her, but something about the client had sounded personal to him on some level. When she'd asked, he had dismissed the question by moving on to the next topic.

A little jaunt on the Internet last night hadn't provided Nora with any sort of personal connection between the client and the Colbys, but her instincts were buzzing with the idea that there was something beneath the surface. This was more than just another case. A lot more.

Maybe her new partner had a little inside info. At this point she didn't see any reason for him not to share. "Does the Colby Agency generally take cases with such a personal connection?"

Tallant turned from his surveillance of the blonde to stare with no small amount of frustration directly at Nora. "We've gone over the strategy for this assignment." He thrust his half-empty glass at her. "Don't ignore check-in time," he reminded as she took the glass. Then he walked away.

Nora glared at the glass, then at his back. She was to check in with him every hour when they were separated. No exceptions.

This…no, *he* was going to be a major pain in the butt.

Nora caught a passing waiter and placed the tumbler on his tray, then smiled appreciatively.

Time to interject her own strategy into this game. He hadn't specifically said she couldn't.

When Tallant was fully engaged in conversation with the *other woman,* Nora headed for the bank of elevators in the glamorous lobby.

The Colby Agency had their way of doing things. But in Nora's opinion there were far more direct methods. She stepped onto the elevator and selected the twelfth floor. Leaning against the back wall of the empty car, she clutched her satin purse close to her chest. Traveling via commercial airliner these days made it difficult to carry one's tools of the trade. But she had devised methods for getting around the possibility of her checked bag being inspected. Incorporating various listening devices and breaking-and-entering tools into her jewelry, cosmetics and such worked like a charm every time.

On the twelfth floor she exited the elevator car and strolled to room 1221. Dr. Vandiver was having a drink with friends in the lobby bar downstairs. According to the waiter serving his table, the group had ordered an appetizer from the restaurant next door. He wasn't going anywhere.

Nora surveyed the door to his room. He would never know she'd been here. With a quick glance right, then left, she gingerly plucked the access card from her purse and slid it into the electronic lock. A small wireless scanner about the size of a makeup compact flashed red, then yellow and finally green. The light on the door's lock went to green. Nora opened the door, simultaneously removing the access card from the locking mechanism.

And she was in.

When the door had closed with a soft click behind her, she surveyed the suite. Same layout as the one she had two floors below but far larger and grander. Management likely ensured that Vandiver always got a VIP suite. Unlike Nora's small sitting room, this one was immense, with a generous balcony overlooking the famous Strip. The first of three telephones sat on a table next to an elegant sofa. Less than a minute was required to place the bug in the cordless handset.

A dozen steps across the plush carpet and she entered the well-appointed bedroom with its enormous bed piled with lush bedding. Vandiver's luggage stood near the walk-in closet, untouched as of yet. The luxurious bed, flanked by wide tables and proud lamps, and a distinctive highboy-style chest of drawers lined the walls not adorned with exquisite art or imposing windows. Two lush chairs, separated by another gleaming ornate table, stood in front of a floor-to-ceiling, wall-to-wall window framing a gorgeous view of the miles of bold, brash architecture and exotic lights that set Sin City apart from any other.

The second phone, on the table to the left of the bed, was the next target. Her fingers moved deftly as she installed the tiny device. The third phone was in the en suite bathroom. Yards and yards of sleek marble and state-of-the-art fixtures cloaked the room. Thick white towels hung on warming racks.

A few seconds more and her work was done.

Nora made her way back to the sitting room and paused long enough to sync her cell phone with those in the room by putting a call through directly to the room. She slid the phone back into her crowded clutch purse and headed for the door.

Tallant would be wondering where she'd gotten off to. She was supposed to be hanging out in the bar, watching Vandiver.

Her accomplishment here would do a hell of a lot more good than watching the guy sip Scotch and nibble at finger foods.

She had no intention of spending any more time than absolutely necessary on this assignment with Tallant. The sooner she was back in Chicago, the happier she would be. Her rotation with him would be over and her next assignment would be with someone else.

Anyone else would be fine by her.

The shadow of his tall frame flitted across her mind's eye. She shook off the distant yearning that accompanied the image.

No man had ever gotten to her in such an annoying manner. The vague idea that she was deeply entrenched in denial frustrated her all the more.

She didn't like him. End of story.

At the entry door she reached for the handle; the distinct hum of the electronic lock stopped her dead in her tracks.

An even more distinct click warned that someone was about to enter the room.

She flattened against the wall just in time for the door to open. It stopped mere centimeters from her nose. Nora held her breath.

"Yes, I'm aware of the consequences."

Vandiver strode across the room, his cell phone pressed against his ear in one hand, the other working his tie loose from his throat.

Nora remained stone still, her lungs bursting to draw in more air, as he wandered left toward the bedroom, still struggling with the knot in his tie and speaking firmly to the person on the other end of the line.

"That's out of the question," Vandiver snapped as he disappeared into the bedroom.

Nora dared to breathe.

She had to get out of here before he came back into the sitting room.

Tallant would kill her if she got caught.

Holding her breath once more, she reached toward the door handle.

The spray of water in the bathroom stalled her escape once more.

Vandiver was preparing to take a shower.

That could work to her benefit in a very big way. If he'd left his cell phone in the bedroom…she could add a device to it, as well.

What a break that would be.…

Tallant's voice rang in her ears. *Don't make a single move without my approval.*

Okay, so maybe he had warned her not to formulate her own strategy.

Nora blinked. She'd certainly already barged past that line in the sand.

What was one more infraction?

Especially if it served to resolve this case.

The move was a risk, no doubt.

If she was caught, she would simply

have to wing it. She'd done it before. Would likely do it again.

Go for it.

She slipped off her stilettos and left them at the door. Her steps silent on the thick carpet, she moved quickly toward the bedroom. As she drew nearer, the water sounds grew louder.

Vandiver started to sing.

Not well and certainly not in tune, but providentially loudly.

Three steps into the room and she hesitated. The door to the bathroom was open.

A couple of her favorite curse words flitted through her mind.

Along with a pair of black trousers, a white shirt and a red power tie, the cell phone lay on the bed, as if he'd tossed it there…as if he had nothing at all to worry about.

Adrenaline moved through her veins. Nothing but Nora Friedman. A smile tilted her lips.

Seven feet stood between her and the phone. She glanced at the bathroom door. The glass-enclosed shower had fogged with the billowing steam.

She could do it.

Piece of cake.

Feet wide apart, she braced for the move.

Her purse vibrated. Her fingers clenched around it as if that would somehow stop the insistent tremor.

Her muscles tightened.

Tallant was checking up on her.

Another glance toward the bathroom.

Just do it.

Three long, soundless strides put her at the foot of the bed. She snatched up the phone and backed up, taking the same number of steps.

The off-key melody wafting from the bathroom assured her that Vandiver remained occupied, allowing her to focus on removing the back from the phone. She dug through her clutch for the tiny device required to do the job. With the purse under her arm once more, she installed the electronic splitter in the phone.

Oxygen didn't fill her lungs again until the back was on the phone and she prepared to toss it onto the bed.

It rang.

Her eyes widened and her heart practically stopped as the phone's raging tune blasted a second time.

Heated oaths resonated from the bathroom.

Move!

Nora tossed the cell phone onto the bed just as it erupted into musical notes again. Without a glance in the direction of the shower, she dashed back to the entry door and snatched up her waiting shoes.

"Yeah."

Vandiver's voice. He was out of the shower and on the phone.

If he heard the click of the door latch disengaging...

His voice grew muffled.

He'd walked back into the bathroom.

Her knees wobbled just a little with relief.

She held her breath, wrapped her fingers around the door handle and pushed downward.

The click of the lock disengaging echoed like an explosion in the air.

Nora slipped into the corridor, slowly let the door close and the lock reengage. With a liberating sigh, she backed up a step.

Clear. She'd accomplished her mission.

Strong fingers wrapped around her forearm.

Her gaze collided with furious gold eyes.

Tallant dragged her several strides down the corridor before leaning his head close to hers and demanding, "What the hell were you doing in Vandiver's room? No." He shook his head. "I don't even want to know."

Busted. "Looking through his briefcase."

Sounded good. But from the ruthlessness of his grip and his continued march toward the stairwell exit, he wasn't buying it for a second.

When he'd pushed through the stairwell door, with her in tow, he surveyed the landing as well as the stairs going in both directions. Confident they were alone, he pointed an outraged face at hers. "I don't know what the hell you were thinking, but we had this talk, Friedman."

They had indeed.

"And I clearly remember thinking it was totally ridiculous at the time." Not the right thing to say, judging by the way his jaw clamped hard and his lips thinned into a flat line of fury.

He was totally ticked off.

The cool tile floor beneath her bare feet served as a harsh reminder that she had taken a huge risk.

He would likely report her to his superiors. Who would in turn convey the entire incident to her boss, Jim Colby.

She was dead.

The great idea didn't seem so great at the moment. Except she had accomplished her goal…assuming he gave her the chance to explain.

"I'm lead on this assignment," he said, his voice low and lethal. "You will follow my orders or you will go back to Chicago."

Funny, she'd never noticed how those thick curls of his swept across his forehead. Gave him an almost boyish look. But there was nothing boyish about his grip or his gaze. He was madder than hell.

"You were tied up with the blonde," she offered humbly, innocently. "The opportunity presented itself and I jumped at it. Isn't that what you wanted me to do?" She widened her eyes, tried her best to look sincere. "Did I misunderstand?"

"Yeah, right." He released her arm only to grab the purse dangling from her right hand.

He opened it.

There would be no explaining that away.

"You just happened to be carrying all this—" he opened the clutch as wide as possible to display the contents for her perusal "—when that lucky break occurred?"

Nora leaned to the right and tugged one shoe on, then leaned the opposite way and pulled on the other. "I like to be prepared, Tallant. Don't they teach you that at the Colby Agency?"

She doubted breaking and entering was a part of the orientation at the Colby Agency. The whole staff was a little uptight for Nora's taste.

He shoved the purse back at her. "Let's go," he ordered.

Her gaze narrowed with suspicion. "Where?"

"Time for a conference call."

The man didn't waste any time. She'd give him that.

"Look here, Tallant." She had no idea

how she would do it, but she had to convince him to go with the flow on this one.

"What?" he growled.

Her purse vibrated.

Surely it was too soon for... She opened her purse, stared at the screen on her phone.

A call to Vandiver's room phone.

Nora held up a hand for Tallant to wait as she opened her phone. Two more rings buzzed before Vandiver answered the call.

"Ten p.m. Your contact will meet you at the Parisian Hotel, under the Eiffel Tower. Bring half the cash and a photo."

Male voice. No detectable accent.

"What does this contact look like?" Vandiver wanted to know. His voice sounded strained...nervous.

"Don't worry," the unidentified man said. "The contact will recognize you."

The caller dropped off the open line.

Vandiver swore, then hung up.

Cash and a picture.

Nora closed her phone and lifted her gaze to Tallant's. "Ten o'clock tonight. He's bringing cash and a photo to a contact."

Understanding dawned in her partner's eyes.

It was going down.

And she had gotten the heads-up.

She savored his stunned expression. "That, Mr. Play-by-the-Rules, is how it's done."

Chapter Four

Friedman was out of control.

Ted paced his room.

His so-called partner sat on the sofa, acting as if he was the one who'd done something stupid.

For the last half hour he'd contemplated calling Victoria.

But…Friedman had garnered a major lead.

Less than twenty-four hours on-site and she had a serious lead.

He'd scarcely made any headway with the alleged mistress.

But then he hadn't broken two laws, one being federal, in the process.

"You're overreacting."

When he whipped around, he fully intended to glare at her with all the frustration and impatience twisting inside him. Didn't happen. Instead his traitorous gaze zeroed straight in on those long, toned legs, one crossed over the other, where the hem of her sleek black dress rested provocatively at the tops of her thighs.

"I am not—" with effort he shifted his focus to her face, which was every bit as distracting "—overreacting." Ted took a breath, ordered his respiration to slow to a more reasonable rate.

He was ticked off, that was all. As if to defy his assessment, his errant gaze wandered back to those shapely legs. Gritting his teeth, he forced his attention upward. He blinked when his eyes committed mutiny once more and stalled on her breasts, encased tightly beneath that slinky black fabric. "We have a certain standard and protocol at the Colby Agency." He managed to look her dead in the eye at that point. "It doesn't include breaking the law unless it's a matter of life and death."

She crossed her arms over her chest and lifted her chin in defiance. "Isn't it? Vandiver is planning to off his wife, right?"

Another deep breath. *Stay calm.* He needed patience here. As much to get his head on straight as to tolerate her attitude. "But the danger is not imminent," he countered, "and the wife is under our protection. Those terms set the tone and pacing of our movements."

The Colby Agency had definitely broken laws in the past; just a few months ago breaking some major ones had been unavoidable. But those instances were the exception, not the rule. "As long as the goal can be accomplished the *right* way, that's the way we do it," he added.

He started pacing again, mostly to prevent staring at any part of her. Around the office she wore slacks and blouses. Not once had she worn anything that drew such attention to her...shape. Was it really necessary for her to be decked out like this now? Clearing the thoughts from his head, he said in conclusion, "I don't understand why that concept is so difficult for you to comprehend."

Standard field operating procedures, client relations, all of this had been gone over time and time again since the merger between the Colby Agency and the Equalizers began. Friedman seemed to be the only one who refused to embrace the ultimate objective.

She stood, planted her hands on her hips, accentuating the perfect curve from that narrow waist to gently sloping hips. "Fine," she announced with obvious disdain. "I got it. Are we going to put together a strategy for tonight or not? Time is wasting."

The set of those full lips told him she was only saying what he wanted to hear. She had no intention of changing her MO, any more than she planned to acquiesce to his lead.

But she was right.

Whether this involved the wife or not,

Vandiver had a clandestine rendezvous to-night, and it was his and Friedman's job to determine the nature of the meeting.

"Unless another call is intercepted," he informed her, "we'll attempt to get close enough to eavesdrop on Vandiver's conversation with the contact. We'll snap a few photos and forward those to the agency for analysis and to Rockford, in case the contact shows up at his location."

Friedman strutted across the room to the wet bar. While Ted struggled to evict from his head the way her hips swayed, she poured herself a double shot of bourbon, neat. He opened his mouth to remind her that Colby investigators didn't drink on the job, but she started talking first.

"That could work." She shrugged. "But if we want to ensure success, we intercept Vandiver. I'll act as the contact. Get the story straight from the horse's mouth while you keep an eye out for the real contact. Distract him or her if necessary."

She was unquestionably out of her mind.

The flash of fury in her eyes warned that he'd stated the thought out loud.

"You have a better plan?" she challenged, then took a long swallow of her drink.

He crossed the room to stand in front of her, took the drink from her hand and set it aside before parking his arms over his chest to match her stance. "First of all, we're here unarmed. We don't know who this contact is. If he or she is local, chances are he or she is armed. In view of the fact that we haven't been able to assess just how desperate Vandiver is, maintaining a cautionary distance is the proper step. We will prepare for that strategy."

Though they weren't armed with weapons, Ted was prepared with the usual intelligence-gathering equipment. All he needed was the place and time—those he had thanks to Friedman—and a proper vantage point for watching and listening. Today's technology provided ample means to gather the necessary information without face-to-face contact.

She glared at the drink he'd set aside and then at him. "That's an option, I suppose." She tilted her face up to his, making him all too aware of just how close they were standing. "But I like my plan better."

"That's irrelevant." He turned away, headed for the bed, where his luggage still lay unpacked, other than the black trousers and shirt he'd selected for making contact with Camille Soto. He dug through the bag and picked out the equipment they would need for tonight. Binoculars. Personal parabolic bionic ear. The lighting in the area would be sufficient so as not to require night vision.

"I should change," she called out to him.

That would definitely make life easier for him.

He strode back to the sitting room as she reached the door. "Give me five minutes and I'll go with you." No way was he letting her out of his sight. She would ditch him and do this her way. He had her number already.

She leaned against the still-closed door and studied him a moment. "I had no idea, Tallant."

Suspicion narrowed his gaze. "What's that supposed to mean?"

She lifted a shoulder and let it fall suggestively. "Considering the way you've been staring at my legs and breasts, I suppose seeing me naked would be entertaining for you."

Fury tightened his jaw. Unfortunately, the images sparked by her statement tightened other areas of his anatomy. "We stick together until this is done."

"Whatever." She pushed off the door, executed a catwalk strut to the nearest chair and plopped down in it, stretching those long legs out in front of her.

He'd asked for that one. Shifting his focus back to business, he gathered the equipment and reached for a summer-weight black sports jacket. The super ear clipped on his belt like a cell phone. He slid the parabolic microphone into his right jacket pocket, the compact binoculars into the left.

Good to go.

He stalked right past her and all the way to the door. When he opened it and paused for her to precede him, she rolled her eyes and pushed out of the chair. He stared at the ceiling as she waltzed past him. This new turn of events was obviously a very bad cosmic joke.

Or maybe it was merely her determination to ensure he stumbled, giving her the lead.

She could forget about it.

He was in charge.

She would learn that lesson one way or another.

Her room was next door to his. She shot him a look as she inserted the key card and shoved the door inward. Something about the look in her dark eyes warned that she wasn't giving up just yet.

Reluctance miring his step, he entered enemy territory—her room.

The whir of a zipper jerked his gaze

upward—just in time to see the black dress slide down the gentle curves of her body and puddle around the matching black stilettos, which she promptly kicked off.

"I'll only be a minute," she called over her shoulder.

Wearing only a lacy black bra and perfectly coordinated thong, she disappeared into the adjoining bedroom.

Sweat beaded on his upper lip. So she was going to play it that way, was she? His unexpected preoccupation with her feminine assets had given her a whiff of weakness in the competition.

Not going to work. He was only human and certainly not blind. Looking at what she flaunted wasn't a weakness. To the contrary, it was a natural instinct. His being male would not override his professional sense.

He had his orders. She would learn to play by the Colby rules or she would be out the door.

That would make his professional life far less stressful and annoying. Back to normal, to the way things were before the merger.

Then why did he feel as if a rock had just settled in his gut?

No. No. No. He absolutely refused to admit, even to himself, that the woman was growing on him in any capacity whatsoever.

"Ready?"

Ted blinked. The slinky black dress was gone. As were the pointy stilettos. But the new outfit was every bit as disturbing on a purely primal level.

Black formfitting slacks with a matching black scoop-necked silk blouse that molded to her breasts as if she wore nothing at all. Could a person actually wear anything under something that tight?

"You ready or what?" she demanded when he didn't immediately react.

It took two seconds too long for his tongue to catch up with his brain. "Yes."

He opened the door, wondering where the heck she'd managed to stuff her cell phone.

As she sashayed past him and into the corridor, he got an answer to the question. The sandals she sported weren't stilettos, but the chunky heels were sky-high. Leather straps and silver chains wrapped around her ankles. Clipped to a strap on the inside of her left ankle was the black slimline cell phone.

Chances were anyone—males in particular—who caught sight of her wouldn't be looking at her feet. Not by a long shot. Ted mentally kicked himself for staring at her swaying backside.

This was going to be harder than he'd imagined.

Chapter Five

The location was perfect for privacy, slap in the middle of the Strip. Lots of patrons as well as tourists. Easy to get lost in a crowd this size.

Nora strolled along the sidewalk running parallel to the miniature river Seine re-creation. The Eiffel Tower replica, half the size of the original, provided numerous locations for a clandestine rendezvous. Talking Tallant into splitting up for better coverage had been a major pain. He didn't trust her one iota to stick to his plan.

He was smart.

He shouldn't trust her to follow a strategy she wasn't convinced was the best course of action.

She was smarter. Or at least not as attached to the rules.

"Still no sign of the target," Tallant's voice murmured in her earpiece.

"Affirmative," she responded. Tallant hadn't bothered to thank her for the device she'd installed in Vandiver's phones. At nine o'clock sharp a command had been sent to the software to block all communications directly to his cell phone and his hotel room. The move wouldn't prevent a caller from calling his room from a house phone; it would block only calls from outside. But that was no longer an issue since he'd left his room more than half an hour ago.

Nora scanned the crowd. Glitzy evening dresses, jeans and tees. Young and old. Vegas was the hot spot for those from all walks of life seeking a thrilling vacation. Or simply a wide assortment of casinos at which to gamble away their hard-earned cash.

She gave her head a little shake. *Never play a game unless you know how to hedge your bet.* That was her motto. She'd spent enough time here in the past to know how to win. Observe, analyze, then strike. Any other way that resulted in a win was pure luck.

She had never once depended upon luck.

Her gaze zeroed in on the man with the thinline briefcase making his way through the crowd clustered near the entrance to the Eiffel Tower. For a minimal fee one could take the elevator to the top for the best views in the city.

But the only view Nora cared about was of the man dressed in black trousers and a white shirt. The red power tie was like a beacon. She purposely hadn't mentioned to Tallant the clothes she'd seen arranged on Vandiver's bed. She wanted to spot him first.

Removing the earpiece and stuffing it

into her pocket as she hustled in the target's direction, she understood that it would take Tallant mere seconds to spot her and realize what she was up to.

Timing was everything.

If she got to Vandiver first, Tallant would have no choice but to back off, however reluctantly, and allow her move to play out.

But if he intercepted her before she reached the target...she was done. He would have her on a plane back to Chicago first thing in the a.m., and by the p.m. she would be facing a Colby firing squad.

Nora didn't get another good breath until she was right on Vandiver's tail. So close she could smell his exclusive cologne.

She had counted on him being early.

Matching his pace, she moved up beside him and slid her arm around his. "Hello, Doctor." She smiled. His eyes widened with uncertainty. "Let's find a nice, quiet place."

She guided him toward the pool deck and small adjoining café du Parc. The spot came with a phenomenal view of the Eiffel

Tower and plenty of distractions to avoid drawing attention.

A waiter cruised by and Nora ordered drinks.

"I thought you would be a—" Vandiver cleared his throat "—a man."

Nora smiled. "Don't be fooled, Dr. Vandiver. I'm very good at what I do."

As in the photo included with his dossier, Vandiver looked young for his age. Not a sign of gray in his full head of hair and not one wrinkle on his tanned face. She imagined that he kept a personal supply of Botox, along with a state-of-the-art tanning bed. No wasted time at a spa for this man.

He glanced around nervously. "I'm not sure how to begin."

Nora waited until he'd made eye contact once more. "I'm certain you explained your needs to my employer. I'll require the photo and the cash, as promised." He reached for the briefcase at his feet as she continued. "We'll review the most relevant details."

He passed the briefcase to her. "It's all there," he said. The line would have been cliché if not for the fact that this was clearly his first time being involved in a deal such as this. He was far too nervous to be anything but a novice. "The photo's there, too."

A quick peek at the photo confirmed that his wife, Heather, was the mark. Confusion lined Nora's brow as she glanced at the envelope containing the cash. Not exactly a beefy bundle.

She set the case at her feet, then scooted it forward, out of sight under the table. "You're sure the money is right?" A guy like him could surely afford the best when it came to hiring a hit man—or woman—for the job of offing his wife.

"Yes." His head moved up and down with enough momentum to make the single word quiver. "Five thousand, just as I was instructed. The rest when…the job is completed."

A ten-thou hit? She wouldn't even take

the job for that price and she wasn't exactly a specialist in the field of assassination.

Whatever. "All right then."

The waiter arrived with their drinks. She smiled in dismissal and he hurried away without the usual barrage of questions about appetizers and such.

"Let's go over the details," she suggested.

He reached for his glass but apparently changed his mind and dropped his hand back into his lap. "I'm in love."

Oh, yeah. She really wanted to hear this. Before she could tell him that it wasn't necessary to divulge an account of his infidelity, he continued.

"I know it's wrong." His chest puffed, then deflated with a long, deep breath. "But my wife is…indifferent to me. She has been for years."

Cry me a river. "There's always divorce," she said before she could recall the words.

Those bedroom blue eyes searched hers. Ironically she couldn't deny the pain she saw in his. "I know. But she refuses to discuss that option." This time he grabbed his glass and downed a hefty portion of the Scotch. She'd ordered what he appeared to prefer based on what she'd observed in the bar earlier.

In an effort to put him at ease, she sipped her wine, then asked, "The property state laws?"

He set his drink aside, those long, perfect fingers still curled around the glass. His hands looked soft and delicate. She doubted he had ever manicured a lawn or even washed his six-figure vehicle.

"I don't know why that would be an issue," he denied with a shake of his head. "She knows I'm more than willing to give her half of everything. It belongs to her as much as it does to me."

Nora was utterly confused now. But whatever. "Would you like any input on how this goes down?"

Even Botox couldn't prevent the line that formed between his eyebrows. "I'm…not sure what you mean." He downed another gulp of Scotch. "I've never done this before. Hired someone...like you, I mean."

Tell me something I don't know. "Are there activities in which your wife regularly participates? Particularly any ones that carry significant risk? Places she goes routinely? Is she prone to accidents? A reckless or careless driver?"

"Oh." The word echoed with mounting confusion. This guy really was nervous. "I think I see what you're getting at."

Nora doubted it.

Three tables behind Vandiver a new guest settled into a chair.

Tallant.

Fury radiated all the way across the expanse separating him from Nora.

She flashed him a triumphant smile and redirected her attention to Vandiver.

"Yoga and Pilates are on Mondays and Thursdays," he recited. "She takes an art class on Wednesdays." He stared at the glass he was turning with those skilled surgeon's fingers. "The spa on Friday. She says it relaxes her." He shrugged. "She's not involved with any groups or even friends. That I know of."

"That may work to our advantage," Nora offered to keep the conversation going.

"Look..." Vandiver studied Nora, his expression pinched with uncertainty and pain, as if he were about to break down. "I suppose I'm not allowed to know your name. But I've done everything I know to do and nothing makes her happy. She just won't be satisfied. I think she wants me to suffer." He looked away. "At least that's what I thought until a few days ago."

Something was wrong here, besides the obvious that the man intended to hire someone to kill his wife. "What happened a few days ago?"

"She changed." His gaze lit on Nora's once more. "Suddenly I couldn't do anything wrong. I was perfect. She insisted we go out to dinner at a place where the friends we used to have go out. She couldn't keep her hands off me. Bragged to everyone she saw how wonderful I was and how our anniversary was approaching."

"Maybe she's decided that the marriage is worth salvaging?" Nora had never met the woman but his story didn't mesh with someone so certain that her husband intended to kill her.

He sighed. "I wish I could believe that."

"You would be willing to attempt an amicable resolution?" Now that was straight-up bizarre.

Annoyance sent his eyebrows into a collision over the bridge of his nose. "Haven't you been listening? Of course I would be! This is beyond insane! I go to sleep next to her every night terrified that I won't wake up the next morning. Do you have any idea how incredibly difficult that is?"

Though she wouldn't tell him as much, she actually did. Five years ago she'd been in exactly that position. Right here in Vegas in fact.

"I'm certain it's very difficult." Time to cut to the chase. "That's why we're here tonight."

He nodded. "I can't live with the

uncertainty anymore." He squared his shoulders. "That's why I decided to take action. My friend, the only one I have left, is an attorney and he suggested I take this route."

Nora blinked. She couldn't have heard that part correctly. "You discussed *this* with your attorney?" Was the man out of his mind?

"Certainly." His expression provided clear evidence that he had no idea why she considered the step so strange. "I don't do anything without consulting my attorney first. I have too much to lose."

"Your attorney advised you to take this step." She needed to make absolutely certain they were talking about the same thing. "To hire someone like me."

"He insisted. She's left me no choice. I can't keep living this way."

Nora resisted the impulse to throw her hands up in surrender and to look for the hidden cameras. This had to be a joke. An episode of some bad reality show.

Vandiver leaned forward, glanced

around, then whispered, "This is not only terrifying, but it's humiliating."

She supposed she could see that. What man wouldn't be afraid of getting caught hiring an assassin to murder his wife? Likewise, what man, an elite surgeon at that, would want the world to know that he couldn't control his own wife?

"I understand, Dr. Vandiver." She forced her expression into one of understanding. "Why don't we move on to the final stage of our strategy and put this behind us once and for all."

He straightened, glanced around again at the other patrons, as if he feared everyone around him understood exactly what he was up to. "I want her watched 24/7. As soon as you've confirmed what I believe she's up to, then we'll take the next step."

Nora nodded despite the fact that she didn't understand why he wanted to put off the inevitable. What was the point?

"My friend, the attorney, has a close contact in the D.A.'s office. We'll take your findings to him and he'll take care of the rest."

Nora's hands went up stop-sign fashion before her brain could suppress the action. "The D.A., as in the district attorney?"

"It's the only way to stop her," he argued, his voice a harsh whisper. "If she's trying to kill me, that's conspiracy to commit murder."

Shock radiated through Nora's bones. Okay. She had to proceed with caution here. This was not at all how she'd expected this conversation to go. "You have evidence that your wife is planning to or attempting to kill you? Is that what you're saying to me?"

Huddling close again, he whispered, "There was a gas leak in our home. The repairman said the valve couldn't have come loose on its own."

The gas leak.

"Were you home?" His wife had insisted he had gone to work, that *she* was the one left at home to perish.

"I was supposed to be at home that day,"

he explained without another covert look around. "But one of my patients had complications. I had to spend the entire morning at the hospital."

"Anything else?" Nora recognized the disbelief in her voice; she only hoped he didn't.

"The brakes went out in our car," he shared. "The mechanic said the line had been tampered with."

"Is that the car you drive to work?" Nora dared a glance in Tallant's direction. He was not going to believe this.

"Generally," he confirmed, "but that week she needed the car and I drove the SUV."

"So," Nora continued, "any other instances you believe are relevant?"

He shook his head.

"Perhaps your wife is trying to kill herself." Sounded that way to Nora. She had the brakes tampered with in the car, the one he generally drove, and then she needed the *car*. If she had prompted the gas leak, after he'd left for work, she could certainly have taken care of it.

He shook his head again. "No. I'm telling you," he reiterated, "my wife is trying to kill me."

Chapter Six

"Rockford's running a check on all Heather Vandiver's communications the past three months," Ted informed Friedman. "He's checking with a contact on where she's been according to her vehicle's GPS. That probably won't help but it will let us know if she's been going someplace regularly that isn't in her usual routine."

Friedman had stripped off the high heels but still wore the supertight outfit. "Rocky'll find out what she's been up to." She jerked her head toward the wall separating her room from his, where they'd tucked Dr. Vandiver for now. "If she's got plans for her cheating husband, he'll get the truth out of her."

Ted wasn't sure that was a good thing. The Equalizers were known for tactics, especially during a critical situation, that fell somewhat below Colby Agency standards of interrogation. "Ms. Soto should be here in the next five minutes."

"That should be interesting." Friedman settled on one end of the elegant sofa that served as the focal point for the sitting room.

"That's your cue to go next door," Ted reminded, fully aware that she knew the strategy they had discussed. He'd learned really fast that she liked pushing the limits—his limits in particular.

"You sure you can handle her alone?" Friedman asked as she pushed to her feet once more. "She could be involved in all this beyond being the other woman. There's always the chance she's on the edge. Dangerous maybe."

The only danger Ted could see was the one right in front of him. "You keep

Vandiver company. I'll take care of inter-
rogating the lady."

Friedman arrowed him a skeptical look.
"Lady?"

Ted opened the door and jerked his head
toward the corridor. "I'll be watching," he
reminded. "Don't do or say anything you'll
regret."

Friedman strolled toward the open door
but paused directly in front of him. "Who's
going to watch you?" she asked in a throaty
voice that made him think of hot sex.

Before he could dredge up a response,
she was out the door.

What was up with this sudden fasci-
nation he had with looking at her? With
inventorying her every asset? Since she'd
started showing up at the office, he'd been
able to ignore how she looked…for the
most part.

Had to be post-traumatic stress syn-
drome. Spending more than twenty-four
hours with her had clearly had an adverse
effect.

Ted secured the door and moved to

the wet bar, where he'd set up his laptop. While Friedman had persuaded Vandiver to relocate to the room next to hers, Ted's room, he had installed the necessary surveillance devices to keep watch on the allegedly worried doctor.

The sound was muted since Soto was due to arrive any moment. Ted watched as Vandiver opened the door and Friedman glided into the room. The woman's movements were as fluid as fragrant oil slipping over bare skin. Ted shook his head. How had he not noticed that before? Working too hard to avoid her, he supposed.

The woman was good. He had to give her that. Not only had she trumped him by going straight to Vandiver when he'd ordered her not to, but she had somehow persuaded him to buy into her cover one hundred percent. Now that was talent.

That whole deception thing again.

How did a man ever trust a woman like that?

Friedman had convinced Vandiver that her people were looking into his concerns regarding his wife while she would serve as his personal protection—no extra charge. Vandiver had bought the story without a second's hesitation. He appeared genuinely desperate to know the truth. Just as desperate as his wife had when she'd contacted Victoria about her husband. Rockford was, thus far, equally convinced that the wife was legitimately concerned for her own well-being.

Victoria had been brought up to speed on this latest turn of events. She, too, was puzzled and had assured Ted that she would do some follow-up of her own.

His gut instinct was sounding a distant alarm. This looked more and more like a game of bait and switch. Lure the attention in one direction while the real trouble went down in the other.

The only question was, who was playing the game?

A rap on the door drew him in that direction and away from surveillance of the activities next door. Friedman had proven she could take care of herself.

But then…that was precisely why he should be worried.

The blonde at the door wore the same tailored black suit she'd worn earlier on the gaming floor. Her eyes were wide with worry. "Where's Brent?" She cleared her throat. "Dr. Vandiver. I checked his suite. He's not there. I tried calling his cell but it went straight to voice mail. Is he all right?"

"Come in, Ms. Soto."

She checked the corridor on either side of her, then moved quickly into the room. He could understand her anxiety, but did she have reason to fear someone might be watching?

He'd soon find out.

"We talked earlier this evening," she said, turning to face Ted. "I thought you were a guest…just visiting." She made no attempt to disguise the accusation in her voice.

Whatever she knew or thought, her anxiety and concern were genuine.

"That's correct," he said, gesturing to the sofa, "in part."

She perched on the edge of the sofa. "I don't understand. Where is Brent?"

To put her at ease, Ted took a seat in the chair to her left. "He's safe."

Camille Soto blinked. "What does that mean? Was there an accident? He said he had a meeting."

"If there had been an accident," Ted offered evenly, "the police would be speaking to you now."

Her stiff posture relaxed marginally.

"Are you aware that Dr. Vandiver and his wife are in a bit of an awkward situation?" He didn't want to feed her information. He wanted her to spill what she knew or suspected.

"Yes." Her voice trembled. "We…we've been having an affair for several months now. He said his wife refused to give him a divorce."

Ted picked up a document from the table that stood between them. "Did he also tell you—" he pretended to review the page "—that he intended to be rid of her one way or another?" Ted zeroed his scrutiny in on the lady. "That he'd hired *someone.*"

Her hands fidgeted in her lap. "Certainly not. He would never even think such a thing. That's something his wife would do. She's unstable."

"The two of you have met?" The wife hadn't said anything about confronting or meeting the other woman. Interesting that she would opt to leave such a significant fact out of the background material she had provided to Victoria.

The blonde nodded. "She came here… once."

"Do you recall the date?" Ted prepared to make a mental note.

"About two weeks ago." Camille Soto wrung her hands now, the enormous rock on her left ring finger an obstacle to her apprehensive movements.

A gift from the doc? he wondered.

"Was there a public confrontation?"

Another concise nod. "I was working.

She made quite a scene." She released a heavy breath. "The whole thing's documented if you'd like to watch the security surveillance recording."

Bingo. Documented. That warning that his instincts had been gearing up to screeched into a full wail now. Something was way off here. "That was the first and only time the two of you have met?" Ted watched her eyes closely as she responded.

She blinked. "Yes." Then she looked away.

The lady wasn't a very good liar. "Did security take care of the incident or was it necessary to call the police?" He had a feeling he already knew the answer before he bothered to ask.

"Security escorted her off the property." Direct eye contact now.

"Did you take any legal action? An order of protection?"

She shook her head, the pain in her expression seemingly real. "I didn't want to embarrass Brent. His reputation is very important to his practice. He could lose clients over that sort of thing."

"Was Dr. Vandiver here when this confrontation occurred?"

"No, thank goodness. He was in New York, at a medical conference."

She'd relaxed substantially since the topic turned to the wife's exploits. "Would you like something to drink?" Now that she had relaxed, he wanted to ensure she stayed that way through a few more key questions. Questions that she might not want to answer.

"No." She looked around the room. "I need to know where he is." She searched Ted's face. "You're sure he's all right?"

He inclined his head and studied her just as intently. "Do you have reason to believe he's in danger?"

Her lips pinched for a time before she answered. "I...told you his wife is unstable."

"You did." He braced for her reaction. "But you are the *other woman*. The chances of hearing a compliment about the wife are slim to none."

She shifted her position on the sofa, reached into her jacket pocket. "I should try his cell phone again. He should have called me back by now."

"You have my word, Ms. Soto." Ted stood. "Dr. Vandiver is safe." He crossed to the laptop. There was no reason not to show her that the doctor was right next door. Ted had gotten all he was likely to at this point.

One point he had gleaned was that all parties involved in this investigation were keeping secrets.

The image on the screen sent adrenaline firing through his veins.

"He's still not answering."

Ted ignored her comment.

He was at the door in three rapid strides.

The blonde called after him as he bounded into the corridor but he didn't look back.

The door to his room stood wide open.

Moving cautiously, he eased into the room, where Friedman was supposed to be babysitting Vandiver.

Deserted.

Ted had been right next door. Separated by one thin wall.

There hadn't been a sound.

No scream.

A tumbler of Scotch sat on the table in front of the sofa. Friedman's purse lay on the bar.

All was exactly as it should be except for one thing.

The overturned chair said all that Ted needed to know.

Friedman and Vandiver had not left of their own free will.

Chapter Seven

"Get her in the car."

Nora didn't relent in her struggle. She glared at the ape attempting to shove her into the backseat next to Vandiver. Let him see her determination.

"Now!" his buddy roared from across the top of the car.

The jerk crushing her arm rammed the muzzle of his weapon into her rib cage. "Get in."

Like he was going to kill her.

"Make me," she tossed back, showing no fear.

Fear equated to weakness.

Weakness would get her killed even faster.

A furtive glance at the guy waiting at the driver's side door confirmed her assumption.

They weren't going to kill her or Vandiver…yet.

Not that she was a mind reader, but she'd heard the one who appeared to be in charge say that their orders were to bring her in undamaged. Maybe Vandiver didn't matter.

Just as the guy's attention shifted back to her, she plowed upward with the heel of her left hand, connecting with his Adam's apple.

He stumbled back, gagging and choking.

She tore free of his grip and reached for his weapon.

The very idea that they'd come here unarmed. The Colby rules were nuts!

Her head jerked back from the abrupt, cruel grip in her hair. "Drop the weapon and get in the damned car," the jerk in charge spat against her ear. The muzzle of his weapon jammed into her skull to emphasize his fierce statement.

"All you had to do was ask nicely." She unclenched her fingers and let the weapon bounce on the concrete floor of the parking garage.

The brute purposely bumped her head against the roof of the car as he shoved her into the backseat. She winced. *Bastard.*

The front doors slammed shut and the tires squealed as the car lunged like a rocket out of the parking slot. They'd backed into the spot closest to the elevator for a fast getaway.

Nora rubbed at her head. Any minute now, if not already, Tallant would realize they were gone and he would give pursuit.

Without a weapon. Dumb. Dumb. Dumb.

She scowled at the creeps in the front seat, dressed like Wall Street execs, driving a European luxury sedan. Weapons kept hidden until there was no choice but to show excessive force.

Not like any P.I.s she'd ever encountered.

Who gave the order to ensure she was unharmed? Who were these guys?

Trouble, she mused, that was for sure.

"What's happening?" Vandiver whispered.

She turned to face him, nose to nose since he was leaning toward her. Not that he'd intended to get so close. The driver had taken the time to blindfold him before shoving him into the car. That they hadn't bothered to do the same to her spoke volumes about intent. Mostly vis-à-vis her.

Another bad sign.

"Hold on," she whispered back, frustrated as hell—mostly at herself for letting these nimrods get them in the car. Seemed it wasn't her night, after all. "Let me get my crystal ball and I'll tell you exactly what's going on."

The doctor's face had paled despite his store-bought tan and the blindfold that covered a good portion of it. The pallor had slid all the way down his throat. "What do they want?"

They'd been abducted. Couldn't be good any way you looked at it. Still, she had an assignment and she wasn't about to let Tallant get a heads-up on her. "You tell me, Doc. Maybe these are the guys your wife hired."

His sharp intake of breath told her he hadn't even thought of that. Maybe she was crazy, but if, as he'd insisted, he was truly worried about his wife's plans for him that would have been the first thought to cross his mind. She stared straight ahead, shook her head. "That's what I thought."

He clammed up like the latest fresh catch on the dinner menu.

"What do you want?" she demanded of their hosts. She had no intention of sitting back here and waiting to see what happened.

"You'll know soon enough," the driver said with a vicious glare in the rearview mirror.

So much for straight talk. She'd keep her eye on the shorter guy—the one in the front passenger seat who'd let her tag-team his weapon. He was the weaker of the two. For sure the least experienced. All she needed was one more opportunity before they got where they were going.

She glanced at Vandiver, who'd caved without so much as a struggle. He would be on his own if he didn't have the guts to make a run for it.

Yeah, and Jim Colby would have her hide when she got back to Chicago.

Twenty minutes later they had left the Strip behind for the unending road that seemed to disappear into the dark desolation of the desert.

They had patted down both her and Vandiver. Taken his wallet and cell phone. Her purse was in the room. If she hadn't tossed the communications link Tallant had given her that could help. She had nothing. Damn it.

Wait.

Vandiver's cell phone was up front with the two goons.

A smile pushed the corners of her mouth upward. All Tallant had to do was activate the tracking software of the communications interceptor she'd added to Vandiver's cell phone and he could track their movements.

As if the driver had read her mind, he picked up the cell phone in question, removed the battery, then threw both out the window.

Dark or no, when the driver made the next right, recognition flared deep in Nora's brain.

Hope…certainty…bravado…all of them drained as surely out of her as if her throat had been sliced.

She knew this place.

Whether she gasped or stiffened, she couldn't say, but whatever she did, Vandiver was suddenly leaning toward her again. "What?"

"Shut up!" the short guy growled.

Just as well. She didn't need Vandiver

freaking out on her and he probably would if she told him they were as good as dead. The guy's hands weren't even tied and he hadn't once reached up to attempt removing his blindfold. No way this guy could be planning to kill his wife. He was way too lightweight for that.

The long drive was lit only by the moon. As they rounded the final curve, the mansion came into view. The barren landscape and soaring mountains around the massive fortress were lit up like a lost piece of the Vegas Strip that had somehow ended up out here in the middle of nowhere.

Sweat dampened her skin as the towering gates opened, beckoning them into the enemy's lair.

Why couldn't this bastard be dead?

Why hadn't someone grown a backbone and put a bullet straight through his arrogant head?

Just her luck.

Karma or something equally annoying.

She'd stepped on too many toes. Used too many people when the need arose.

Now she would pay the price.

The car stopped and she reached for the door. No point waiting for the shortest of the two apes to drag her from the backseat.

The business end of a handgun flew up to her face. "One wrong move and I'll have to disobey orders," her escort warned. He'd jumped out of the front passenger seat and leveled his weapon before she'd had time to open the door and get one foot on the ground.

Evidently he'd dredged up a little courage during the doomed ride.

"Do I look stupid to you?" she demanded, resisting the urge to roll her eyes.

The driver ape had wrenched Vandiver from the car. This time the poor guy resisted.

Too little, too late.

He shouldn't bother.

Barring a flat-out miracle, they were toast.

As they climbed the front steps, memories

of the last time she was here flickered like a bad movie reel in her head. Falling down those stone steps. Rolling onto her back and putting a bullet right between the eyes of one bodyguard. A shot to a kneecap of another. Then she'd scrambled to her feet and run like hell, barely making it through the gate as it closed behind the property owner as he drove away.

He'd thought she was dead by the time he cleared the gate. Imagine his surprise when she'd put a bullet into one of the tires of his limo. She'd aimed for the driver and for him, but in the condition she'd been in, she'd missed them both.

She'd eaten the dust left in the wake of the vehicle's frantic departure.

Then she'd grown a brain and run like hell. Luckily a passing car had picked her up before the rest of his security could rally and come after her.

The door opened and a third well-dressed goon stepped back for them to enter.

"Take him downstairs," the guy closing

the door announced. "He's waiting in the study for *her.*"

He.

Yeah, *him.*

Vandiver called out to her in desperation as the short guy dragged him away.

So much for this case.

Tallant was going to be seriously ticked.

The driver jerk manacled her arm and hauled her farther down the long entry hall. Second door on the left. She knew the way. She hadn't needed any directions.

He shoved her through the door, then closed it behind her.

He sat in a leather wingback, a His Majesty's Reserve cigar in his hand. Only the best for the reigning emperor of Sin City.

"It's been a long time, Nora." He puffed the hand-rolled cigar, which cost more than most people earned in a week.

She walked to the closest chair and dropped into it. "Not long enough."

"You look well."

Who else would be wearing a two-thousand-dollar silk suit at two in the morning? Imported leather shoes. Not a hair out of place, though there was more gray at the temples than before.

Only Ivan Romero, the man who owned the largest piece of every casino on the Strip. Sadistic scumbag.

"I thought you'd be dead by now." She relaxcd into the chair.

Those evil brown eyes flickered with scarcely contained fury even as a smile split his deceptively handsome face. "You left me quite a mess the last time you visited my fair city."

His city. Right. She presented him with an equally insincere smile. "I try."

"Why are you here?"

The smile was gone and so was his patience. Time to get down to the nitty-gritty.

"I'm here on business." She folded her arms over her chest and stared back at him with matching frigidity.

"Whose business?"

"Not yours." That would be his foremost concern.

"Shall I ask the question again, *querida?*"

She arched an eyebrow at the disingenuous endearment. "Checking out a cheating spouse," she said, knowing exactly what nerve that would hit.

Fury blazed in his expression just as surely as if he'd spontaneously combusted. "Still making a living prying into the private affairs of others, I see."

Affairs being the key word there. "Why don't we cut to the chase, Ivan? You cheated on, abused and almost killed your wife. I helped her leave you and start a new life with a brand-new identity, which you still can't crack. We've been down this road before. I don't know where she is or what her new name is. That was the deal. I can't divulge what I don't know."

Even the woman's own father didn't know the final details. The two had said their goodbyes ahead of Nora's setting the operation into motion.

Chalk one up for her. Nora resisted the impulse to lick her finger and hold it up in the air.

"I'm well aware that you did your job thoroughly," Romero admitted. "If it was possible to find her, I would have done so by now. I've come to terms with that reality."

"Then why am I here?" This little tête-à-tête seemed like a colossal waste of time to her. Vandiver was likely hysterical. Nora had an investigation to conduct.

"I didn't arrive at this understanding overnight," Romero reminded. "It was slow in coming. When I admitted defeat, I shifted my energies to a different avenue of satisfaction."

Revenge. Yeah, she got it. That was why she was here after all these years.

"Imagine my surprise when you showed up here." He laughed softly. "You always did have perfect timing."

Yeah, yeah. Give her a gold star.

"I've waited five long years for this

moment." He chuckled. "To have you here in my home. Under my dominion."

Did he really believe she would ever be completely under his control? She would die first. Almost had the last time. She'd escaped with a fractured jaw, two cracked ribs and a mild concussion to prove it.

"I'm certain you've known my whereabouts the entire time. All you had to do was call and we could've had lunch." Why was he beating around the bush? This wasn't his usual style.

"True." He nodded. "I've kept up with your activities to some degree. Not that I had a precise plan for revenge. Not really." He tamped out the cigar, left it in the crystal ashtray. "More a fantasy of sorts."

Oh, now, that was what she'd really wanted to hear, that she was this creep's fantasy on any level. "Wow, I'm flattered."

"Actually." He rested his elbows on the intricately detailed chair arms and steepled his fingers. "I've considered at length the varied and painstaking ways I might teach you a lesson about the choices you've made in life."

"What? You're my father now?" Her pulse rate had adjusted to the threat of the unknown. She was resigned to her fate to some degree, but that didn't mean she was looking forward to it.

"Brace yourself, Nora." He stood, adjusted his elegant jacket. "You're going to experience extraordinary pain. You will wish for death, but it will not come. Then perhaps you'll know how I suffered after you raped my life."

"You know, Ivan—" she pushed out of her chair, not about to give him that position of authority "—you really should get over it. You're just ticked off because someone got away before you were through with them."

"Ah, I see. You thought you were so smart back then. Still do, it seems." He made that annoying, condescending tsking sound. "You're wrong, dear Nora. It wasn't simply a matter of her getting away."

"So she took a small portion of your vast

fortune." She made a scoffing sound of her own. "I'm certain you don't even miss it. In fact, it's rather petty of you to whine over a few hundred thou."

Romero moved a step toward her. As if on cue the door opened and two of his goons moved up behind Nora.

"What she took, dear naive Nora, was by far more precious than money." He sneered at her, sheer hatred glittering in his eyes.

Her senses moved to a higher level of alert. He couldn't possibly know.

"She took my child."

Chapter Eight

2:00 a.m.

"Run that back on visual search." Ted's gut clenched as the tech did as he requested.

The hotel's security system was top-notch. The video footage of the two men entering the room where Friedman and Vandiver had been was clear and crisp. The intruders had used what looked like a hotel key card for access. But Ted was well aware the card could have been acquired elsewhere. Technology could never outrun those determined to breach or otherwise dissect it. Friedman had used a similar technology earlier tonight.

Less than three minutes after entering

the room the two intruders had escorted Friedman and Vandiver to the elevator. Ted was surprised by that. The likelihood that other guests would be on the elevators was great, whereas the stairwells were more often deserted.

The bastards were either damned cocky or felt confident that they had nothing to worry about. That was the most disturbing part.

Ted glanced at the security surveillance booth's open door, where Camille Soto stood just beyond hearing range, deep in conversation on her cell phone. She looked tired and frustrated. Maybe a little scared.

But she hadn't once brought up the subject of reporting the incident to the police. Instead, she'd insisted on seeing what she could learn off the record.

"You want to watch it again?"

Ted pulled his attention back to the screen where the tech had played the same seven minutes over and over. "Once more."

As the four on the surveillance video reached the basement-level parking garage, Friedman had given the guy attempting to force her into the car one hell of a hard time. A smile nudged at Ted's lips. If it hadn't been two against one—two armed men at that—she likely would have gotten away clean.

While Vandiver hadn't resisted in the least. Ted rolled the idea around in his head even as he watched those final moments a fifth time. Maybe the guy was afraid of injuring his hands. Or just afraid.

Soto stepped into the small, gadget-packed room. "The license plate gave us nothing."

The plate had been captured on the video. For the good it had done, apparently. "Thanks for nudging your Las Vegas PD contacts at this hour."

"What do we do now?" Her worried gaze locked on the final frame of the surveillance video and she pressed the back of her hand to her mouth as if to hold back a desperate sound.

Ted gave the tech a pat on the shoulder. "Thanks, man." He gestured to the door. "Why don't we go to your office," he said to Soto.

She nodded, then led the way. They'd been there once already this morning. Ted had more questions. He wanted her in that office, surrounded by all the photos— particularly the two of her and Vandiver together—where her reactions would be less guarded.

Her well-appointed office had a perfect view of the main gaming floor. The glass wall behind her desk was a two-way mirror. She could see those below but all they saw, if and when they peered upward, was reflective glass.

Framed photos and certificates lined another wall. Comfort and luxury were the themes surrounding Ms. Soto's position of authority. A position that not only encouraged but also required that she know her clients as well as her competition. Vegas was a large city, no question, but the world of casino management was small. The players knew each other. Made it a point to become familiar with the each other's associates.

The moment the surveillance video had been played the first time, Ted had noted the recognition in Camille Soto's eyes. She did know the men who'd taken Friedman and Vandiver. The question was, why wasn't she cooperating with Ted? If she wanted her lover back safely, why delay his reaction to the overt move?

Unless there was an agenda she preferred not to share.

He settled into the chair in front of her desk. "I've spoken at length with my colleagues in Chicago," he began. "At this point I believe it would be in Dr. Vandiver's best interest to contact the authorities."

Her eyes widened with fear but she quickly schooled her expression. "But we haven't received a ransom demand. If this is another escapade of his wife's, contacting the police may only end up news fodder."

Dig that hole a little deeper, lady. "But,"

Ted challenged, "you said that Ms. Vandiver's confrontation with you was the only incident of that nature. That being the case, I'm having trouble making the leap to this abduction being her doing."

An unnecessary survey of her office delayed Soto's response. Scrambling for a logical one, he would wager. The idea that she had information that could help Ted propelled his frustration and anger to the next level. But he wasn't ready to play bad cop just yet. If he gave her enough rope, she would hang herself.

"It was the only time she confronted me," Soto insisted. "But there have been a couple of times when she hired some bully to threaten him...Brent. No physical altercations, just threats."

"These threats were carried out face-to-face or by phone?" Pushing her to be specific was the quickest way to detect deception.

"Face-to-face...I believe." She checked her cell phone to avoid continued eye contact.

Hard to conceive that she wouldn't know with certainty, considering her relationship with Vandiver. "These confrontations occurred in public settings? At his practice here in Vegas?"

Her gaze met his briefly. "I think so."

"I ask since there might very well be surveillance footage of the incidents—if they occurred in a public place. Perhaps one of the two men who took Dr. Vandiver and my associate was responsible for one or both of the previous confrontations."

"I'm just not sure," she lied. "Brent didn't give me all the details." She moistened her lips and looked Ted straight in the eye. "He wanted to spare me the ugliness his wife initiated."

How thoughtful and convenient. Ted pulled his cell phone from his pocket. "We shouldn't put off contacting the authorities. The first forty-eight hours in an investigation of this nature are crucial."

The pause as he slid open his phone was accompanied by complete silence. His thumb poised over the first digit even as the air in the room thickened with the weight of tension.

"One of the men," she said, drawing his attention away from the keypad and across her desk, "looked kind of familiar… maybe."

Ted closed his phone and probed her gaze with his own. The telltale signs of being cornered were written clearly on her face. "You recognized him?" He prepared to reopen his phone. "All the more reason to make the call."

Outright fear seized her face. "No." She shook her head. "You don't understand." She hesitated, blinked. "If the person behind this is the man I suspect, calling the police will only make things worse."

Ted felt his eyes narrow with mounting doubt. "I'll need his name."

She moistened her lips. "Ivan." A big, shaky breath. "Ivan Romero."

Ted waited for her to continue.

"He owns the Copacabana." Her lips pinched with that mounting uncertainty.

"Among others. He's a very powerful man."

"You're certain these men work for him?" Ted understood there was a lot more she wasn't telling just yet.

Soto nodded. "Ivan called me a few minutes ago."

So that was the call she'd gotten while he was reviewing the surveillance video. "And?" Ted prompted, his patience history.

"He said he had an old score to settle with your associate. That if I didn't call the police, Brent…Dr. Vandiver…would be released unharmed." Another of those quaking breaths. "This has nothing to do with him."

Ted opened his phone and entered Simon Ruhl's number.

"You can't call the police," Soto urged, leaning forward. "Ivan is not a man you want to cross."

Simon answered on the second ring. "I need anything you can find on Ivan

Romero," Ted explained. "We have a situation."

Soto's eyes widened as he related recent circumstances to his colleague at the Colby Agency. When Ted ended the conversation and closed his phone, she shook her head slowly from side to side.

"What've you done?" Her hands shook as she clasped them atop her desk. "You don't understand...."

"I understand perfectly. Simon Ruhl is my colleague at the Colby Agency. Not informing them of this situation was out of the question."

The relief that claimed her expression was palpable. "He won't contact the police?"

"Not as long as I assure him I have the situation under control." There was no time to placate her anxiety. All he needed was her cooperation. "Tell me about Romero." Simon would get back to him with all he could find, but Ted needed whatever the lady had. "Where can I find him?" She'd mentioned the Copacabana. A classy, well-

established casino hotel. But before Ted
went barging into the place and encountered what would likely be top-notch security, he needed inside information. A way
to get to the man outside that setting.

"He doesn't spend much time at the
casinos anymore. He prefers his private
residence."

"Give me the details of his private residence," Ted prompted.

"His personal security is primo," she
said, not exactly answering his question.
"There's a lot I don't know about Ivan. A
lot no one knows. But what I am certain
of is that he isn't someone you want to go
up against. Certainly not alone. I've heard
rumors."

"Rumors?" The phone in his hand
vibrated. A report from Simon had
downloaded.

"The kind," she warned, "that lets me
know that I don't want trouble with him."

"What details do you know about the
security at his residence?" Ted wasn't beat-

ing around the bush anymore. He needed facts. Now.

"Well-trained. They're pros." She shrugged. "Ivan is a very wealthy man. He's not taking any chances. It's a ten-acre compound. He uses cameras and dogs."

Not good news. "You've been there?"

She nodded. "To a Christmas party once. A birthday celebration earlier this year."

Sounded like she knew the guy better than she wanted to let on. "Whose birthday?"

"His."

Oh, yes. There was the guilt. It clouded her expression, as if she'd been caught with the smoking gun in her hand. "Then you must know him quite well."

"As well as anyone in the business, I suppose," she confessed.

"Good." Ted locked his gaze with hers. "Then you won't mind getting me inside."

Soto held up both hands. "That would be impossible."

"No problem." Ted prepared to open his

cell phone. "I'm sure I can find a cop or a fed who isn't afraid of him."

"I'd like to keep my job," she offered, her voice too quiet. "But I want to stay alive a whole lot more."

2:45 a.m.

SIMON'S RETURN CALL SURPRISED Ted. Not simply because he'd already sent a thorough report on Romero, but because the call was actually a teleconference that included Jim Colby. But then, Friedman was a member of Colby's team. Ted shouldn't have been surprised.

"Ivan Romero is bad news all the way around," Colby informed Ted. "He's on several federal watch lists. Drugs. Gunrunning. Human trafficking. Just to name a few. But no one has ever been able to finger him for any of the suspected crime activity."

A volatile mixture of fury and fear trickled into Ted's veins. "Have you been able to establish a connection between him and

Vandiver?" If not, there was every reason to go with Soto's claims. That Friedman had been the target. Vandiver just happened to be in the way. Or perhaps he was collateral to ensure Soto's cooperation, as she'd alleged.

"None. Camille Soto," Simon explained, "worked for Romero prior to taking the position at the Palomino. She knows him better than she's admitted. As far as we can determine, Vandiver doesn't even know the man."

Ted had wandered into the corridor outside Soto's office to take this call. He leaned his head to the right and verified that she remained behind her desk, shuffling through papers. Her landline as well as her cell lay in plain sight on the desktop.

"This isn't about Vandiver or Soto," said Jim, speaking up next. "This is about Nora."

That fury simmering in Ted's blood ignited into a full blaze. "I presume this has something to do with her previous time in

Vegas." Victoria had explained that Friedman had been assigned to this case because of her experience in the Vegas casino world.

"Five years ago Nora worked for Romero," replied Jim.

A frown nagged at Ted's brow. "In what capacity?" he asked Jim.

"It was an undercover operation bankrolled by Romero's former father-in-law."

Ted absorbed the information, worry rising inside him, as Jim Colby laid out the details of Friedman's interaction with Romero five years prior. His wife of three years had finally confirmed what her father had suspected all along: Ivan Romero was a monster. The wife had learned she was pregnant and decided that to protect the child she had to get away from Romero before he learned her secret. The wife's father had looked until he found the best, Nora Friedman, to make it happen.

Friedman had taken it upon herself, after achieving a deep cover status with Romero, to ensure the wife got a little something for her pain and misery. One point five million dollars disappeared with the wife.

Friedman had barely escaped from Romero with her life. A mock federal investigation had kept him from retaliating immediately after her escape. But like all the other times before, he had been cleared of suspicion.

"I can only assume," Jim went on, "that Nora believed Romero had decided to let it go. I was aware she'd worked an investigation in Vegas, but since Romero hadn't attempted to track her down in the past five years, there was no call for concern. This was supposed to be a low-profile assignment."

Intelligence gathering. Ted got that. All involved agreed that going to the authorities was a risk at this point since there was reason to believe loyalty to Romero went deep in the local law enforcement scene. But to go in alone, Ted would need certain assets. "Do you have a contact for me?"

"Yes," Simon confirmed. "He's waiting for you in the lobby bar now. I've sent a photo and background info to your phone. He'll supply you with whatever you need. He carries an entire store in his trunk."

"Use extreme caution, Tallant," Jim advised. "The man who hired Nora to help his daughter escape from Romero died within days of her disappearance."

"Romero killed him?" Didn't bode well for Friedman.

"The death was ruled an accident," Jim clarified. "The man was seventy-five and wheelchair bound. A fire in the middle of the night burned his home to the ground with him inside. A power failure was blamed for the home security system's malfunction. But Nora believes Romero was behind it. Maybe attempted to learn his wife's location."

"We're sending Trinity Barrett as backup," Simon put in. "He'll arrive via the agency's private jet at four-thirty. You must realize that the strategy you outlined is too dangerous to attempt alone, Ted. The chances of success are minimal."

Ted braced for battle. "I can't wait that

long. From what we know about Romero, it may be too late already. Waiting is out of the question."

He had advised Simon of his recovery strategy in their first phone conversation an hour ago. Soto had reluctantly agreed to take Ted there under the pretense of picking up Vandiver. But she had refused to go to the police. If Ted did so, she would deny all that she had told him. She'd already had the surveillance video destroyed.

There was no other option.

An extended pause on the other end had Ted's teeth grinding. He had to get moving. There was no time for debate.

"The decision is yours," Simon said, capitulating with audible reluctance. "We'll do all we can from here. I have a call in to a friend of mine assigned to the Bureau field office in the area."

Ted ended the call. His gaze locked with Soto's. She was watching him, the same defeat on her face that had lodged itself deep in his gut.

If Friedman was still alive, it would be an outright miracle.

Chapter Nine

2:50 a.m.

The walls were concrete. Cold and gray.

Nora turned around slowly, sizing up her predicament.

The cell was about nine by nine with no chair or bed or anything. Just a concrete box. The door had a small window built into it. There were metal bars over the small opening. Not even a knob or handle on the inside of the door.

Romero was a freak.

Nora had known about the tunnels. The wife had told her.

Wife. Brenda. Her name was Brenda. Or it used to be when she was married to the psycho upstairs. Romero had so many enemies and so many black-market activities going on that when he'd purchased the mansion on his stately ten acres, his first order of business had been to have an escape route excavated beneath the house.

To guests of his home, it appeared to provide passage from the private basement game room to the pool and the expansive entertaining area behind the house. But there was a secret passage that led into a trio of tunnels, one of which led to a hidden helipad nearly a mile from the property. Along with the helicopter was an all-terrain vehicle. And weapons.

All the amenities a wealthy, overachieving criminal would want.

Nora hadn't seen Vandiver since he'd been dragged away from her. He could be down here somewhere, but if he was, he was damned quiet. The slightest sound echoed in the endless sea of concrete.

Could be dead, for all she knew. Victoria Colby-Camp would be less than happy, but

Nora wouldn't have to worry about that. She would be dead, too. Whatever Ivan said, he would kill her. He would never let her leave here alive. Tallant would have to deal with the fallout.

She set her hands on her hips and walked around the perimeter of her cell.

Wasn't the worst place she'd been held. The idea that it might be the last ticked her off.

Five years! Romero couldn't have come after her way before now?

No. She shook her head. He'd exhausted every avenue possible to find his wife on his own; then he'd sat back and waited for Nora to grow complacent. And then show up in his city, disarmed.

She hadn't given him a thought in years.

Big mistake.

He'd been lying in wait…like the snake he was. Protecting his territory and waiting for her to wander back into his dominion.

She'd completely dropped her guard where he was concerned.

Seriously big mistake.

Tallant didn't like her at all. She wondered how much trouble he would go to in a rescue attempt. Knowing him and his Colby rules, he'd just call the cops and hasten her demise.

Romero owned the law in Vegas.

No one was going to bust in here and demand to know what he'd been up to. No way.

She executed an about-face and traced her steps in the opposite direction. Then there was the Vandiver case. The wife had insisted her husband was trying to kill her, but now Nora wasn't so sure.

Vandiver appeared convinced that his wife, their client, was trying to kill him.

Tallant could deal with that. Besides, Rocky was in Los Angeles with the missus. He would get the truth out of her. The Equalizers and the Colbys were vastly different when it came to getting to the bottom line.

If Rocky were here in Vegas, he would find a way to reach Nora before it was too late. No one or nothing would stand in his way. Not even the law.

Just her luck to be stuck with Tallant.

Her feet stalled. He'd given her credit for her strategy to get to Vandiver. Maybe he wasn't that bad. And she'd caught him looking at her in a way that had surprised her. It was possible, she supposed, that he liked her more than he wanted her to know.

But did he respect her investigation skills?

Truth was she'd been denying a physical attraction to him since day one. No use denying it now. It wasn't like she would live to regret allowing the thought.

Maybe that was why she'd been so determined to make sure he respected her ability as an investigator.

She looked around the box again. Okay, there was a slight chance she'd overrated her skills.

After all, she was in here and Tallant was out there.

Could be he had a point about strategy.

"Nah." This was just bad timing. Bad timing and ancient history.

Nora crossed to the door and tried to see past the bars of the small eye-level opening. Sounded deserted out there. Dimly lit.

Ancient history or not. Bad timing or not.

She was in deep trouble here.

Wait.

She'd surveyed the cell three or four times and hadn't noticed any holes for hidden cameras.

But they would be here. That was one absolute certainty. Romero would be watching every move she made. He would take no chances whatsoever.

"If the mountain won't come to Mohammed," she mumbled as she reached for the hem of her blouse and then pulled it over her head and tossed it to the floor. "We'll

just bring Mohammed to the mountain."
She reached for the waist of her slacks
next.

"WHAT IS SHE DOING?" ROMERO leaned
forward and stared at the screen. Nora had
stripped down to her bra and panties. "You
searched her?" He stared up at the bodyguard towering next to his desk.

"Thoroughly, sir," his most trusted employee, Quinton Lott, insisted. "She has
nothing on her except the clothes."

That now lay on the floor.

Uneasiness slid through Romero. He
knew this woman too well. Far too well.
She could not be trusted on any level. Not
for a single second.

"Check her again," Romero ordered.

"Yes, sir."

The door closed behind his head of
security.

Romero studied the woman on the monitor. Slender, toned. He had wanted her so
badly five years ago. Still wanted her now.

Nora had not changed. If anything, her body was even more appealing.

But he would not have her now any more than he had five years ago. For wholly different reasons this time, of course. This time it was because his relentless desire to watch her suffer far outweighed his lingering wish to ravage her sexually.

This time she would not escape his wrath.

Even as he determined not to be distracted by her antics, she bent at the waist and removed one shoe, then the other. That she held on to the last shoe and inspected the sole sent an alarm shrieking in his brain.

On the monitor, the cell door opened and Lott entered.

Now Romero would see what she was up to.

GREAT.

Nora sized up Lott, Romero's head of security, as he entered her cell.

Big. Mean as hell. Nearly a decade of service to his master.

Would've been nice if the less experienced dope from the car ride here had made an appearance.

"What're you doing?" Lott demanded as he strode toward her, leaving the door open behind him.

Nora shrugged. "It's hot in here. So I took my clothes off."

"Give me the shoe."

She tightened her grip on her right shoe. "It's only a shoe." Too bad it wasn't one of her stilettos. She'd aim for an eye…or maybe a jugular.

He held out his hand as he came closer. "Give it to me."

She had one shot.

She had to be fast.

Faster than a big, muscled-up guy wearing a tailored suit.

"Fine." She reached the shoe toward him.

He wrapped a cruel, indignant grip around it.

She released the shoe.

He made the mistake of inspecting it.

She darted around him. Out the door.

The scrub of his shoes on the concrete echoed right behind her.

She ran harder, had no idea where she was going. She'd only been down here once and that was five years ago.

Faster.

If he caught up with her…

He roared curses behind her…so close she could practically feel his hot breath on her bare back.

Run!

Faster!

She couldn't slow for the fork up ahead.

Right.

She propelled herself to the right. Pushing with all her might.

Go!

The tunnel twisted right again, almost causing her to lose purchase on the cool, damp floor.

Lott was close.

She leaned forward, barely escaping his grappling fingers.

Steps.

Damn!

She lunged up the broad steps. Her chest tightened. Just breathe.

He stumbled. His fingers raked her back.

She propelled herself forward. The palms of her hands hit the step in front of her. She kept scrambling…moving…up. Up! Faster!

"You're dead when I catch you!"

She burst up onto the final step.

Outside. Pool.

She zigzagged around the pool.

Voices shouted in the distance.

Security.

Dogs barked.

Oh, hell. Don't stop! She had to escape the landscape lighting.

A ping echoed around her.

Gunshot.

Wall. Straight ahead.

Oh, God.

Something latched onto her ankle. Teeth buried into her skin. She felt the pain before she heard the growling.

Dog.

She glanced down. Tripped, landed face-first on the ground.

Her jaw clamped down hard to prevent screaming as the feral teeth ground into her flesh.

"Down!"

The dog abruptly released her.

Only then did she become aware of the salty taste of tears on her lips or the thundering beneath her sternum and the jerky spasms of her chest.

Cruel fingers manacled her arms and jerked her upward. Her ankle was on fire.

The men on either side of her twisted her around to face the head honcho.

Lott's palm connected with her jaw. Her head twisted to the right from the force.

"Take her inside," Lott ordered, his face contorted with fury.

The men hauled her forward. She resisted, earning a spree of harsh curses.

By the time they reached the entrance to the kitchen, the adrenaline had receded enough for her brain to fully inventory her injuries.

Chewed-up ankle. The soles of her feet were skinned and raw. Her arms, where the jerks continued to grip her, were bruised. And her face stung from the slap. Too low on the jaw to give her a black eye, but her lip was definitely swelling.

She'd tried. She couldn't just sit back and wait for Ivan to have his way.

"Put her there."

Speak of the devil. She smiled at Romero as he directed that she be placed into a kitchen chair.

He folded his arms over his chest and pointed a stare at her that would have ignited a rain-dampened forest. "You're not escaping me this time," he guaranteed. He nodded to her chest, where her lacy bra showed off her cleavage. "This time I will watch you pay."

"You sure know how to sweet-talk a girl."

Lott reared back his hand to slap her again.

Romero shook his head. "No. When the time comes, I'll have the honor."

"Mr. Romero."

Romero shifted his attention to yet another well-dressed creep who entered the room. This one had shoulder-length blond hair. He whispered something in his boss's ear. Nora watched Romero's face for some indication of the news his associate passed along.

"I'll be right there."

Evidently nothing troubling, since his expression remained calm and unmoved.

To Lott, Romero instructed, "She's tested my patience. If she makes a sound or a move, go ahead and break her neck."

He glared at her once more before exiting the room.

Bastard.

"You heard him," Lott reiterated. "Don't feel as if you're putting me out if you choose to disobey." He rubbed his palms together. "I would love to twist that slender neck of yours until it snaps like a twig."

She ignored the big jerk when she wanted to tell him where to go. Maybe what to do when he got there. But Romero had said she wasn't to make a sound. She'd already pushed his patience to the limit. Having Lott perform a move even a good orthopedic surgeon couldn't undo wasn't exactly her plan A.

A woman's voice filtering in from somewhere in the house silenced Nora's thoughts.

Romero had company?

She strained to listen beyond the goofballs muttering behind her. Romero was railing at someone but she couldn't make out more than a word here and there. Judging by his tone, he was not a happy man.

Lott leaned against the kitchen island, his ugly glower resting fully on her. Nora worked at keeping her face clean of anticipation.

More shouting.

Something was *unacceptable*. Definitely a female. A mad one at that.

Lott moved to the door that led into the main entry hall. Obviously to listen to whatever was going on with his boss.

Nora checked the position of the other two in the room. Still hanging out by the French doors directly behind her.

Just her luck.

The rise of voices, male and female, shattered the low buzz of conversation around Nora. The male voice she recognized as Romero.

The female…Camille Soto!

Did that mean Tallant was here?

Hope swelled in Nora's chest.

She considered Lott's back. If she screamed, would he have time to turn around and shoot her before Tallant got in here?

Definitely.

Break her neck?

Maybe not.

She dared to glance over her shoulder at the two behind her.

No making it outside or into the hall…

Lott abruptly turned, as if he'd heard the thought. Nora's pulse skittered.

Lott motioned for one of the men by the French doors to come to him. Nora watched as the two huddled, Lott passing along instructions she couldn't hope to hear. The other man nodded, then disappeared into the hall.

Was Soto in danger? Were they going to drag her in here, too?

Nora couldn't just sit there and do nothing.

Still, there was one man stationed at the French doors behind her.

Lott crossed to where she sat and manacled her arm. "One word," he reminded with a lethal glare, "and you're dead."

She nodded her understanding. He hauled her to her feet. She winced. More at how sore her arm was from all the manhandling than from the scrapes on her feet or the injury to her ankle.

He forced her out of the kitchen through the French doors. His pal followed. Since she hadn't noticed Lott ordering him to do so, she imagined that the guy followed only to watch her hips sway in the skimpy panties as she walked.

Why not give him a show he wouldn't soon forget?

"Come on," Lott muttered as he dragged her toward the entrance to the underground tunnel beyond the lavish pool and patio.

Back down the cool concrete steps. Along the dimly lit gray corridor.

To the cell where she'd been held before.

Back at square one.

He shoved her into the cell. "Put your clothes on. You wouldn't want your corpse to be discovered naked, would you?"

She made a face at the big, ugly thug.

Taking her time, she dragged on her slacks and blouse. Then the shoes. Hurt like hell with no socks but nothing she could do about that.

After a quick inspection of her ankle, she crossed to the back wall, leaned against it and slid down to the floor.

She needed a new plan. Not that it would stop the outcome of this situation. Even if Tallant had arrived with Soto, the chances of him finding her were about nil. Ivan wanted to torture and to murder.

Odds were that would happen.

But she didn't have to make it easy.

Chapter Ten

"You did exactly as I instructed?" Romero had never known Camille Soto to double-cross him—if he had, she would be dead now—but he had an uneasy feeling about this negotiation.

She nodded firmly. "Yes." She inclined her head and eyed him circumspectly. "Haven't I always followed your instructions to the letter?"

"Of course, but…" He folded his arms over his chest and tapped his chin with his forefinger. "This is a very delicate matter. A personal matter. You're certain this associate of Nora's has no idea where she is?"

"None." She shook her head for emphasis.

"He called his employer and they're going to the police." Soto smiled—the smile that had first drawn his attention when she'd been a mere waitress. "And we both know how that will go."

"Bear in mind, Camille," Romero warned, "that if you do not hold up your end of this bargain where the investigator from Chicago is concerned, I will see that your precious doctor ends up every bit as dead as his vengeful wife wishes him."

"Then neither of us has any reason to be concerned," she insisted.

"You will handle this with Vandiver?"

"Just another attempt on his life by his crazy wife," Soto assured him. "He was very fortunate that you intervened. Sadly, the woman was not so lucky."

"Sadly," Romero echoed. He gestured to the front door. "I'll walk you out."

Camille Soto appeared puzzled.

"He's in the trunk of your car," Romero explained as he ushered her forward. "Blindfolded and secured. When you arrive back at the Palomino, you explain how you and I acquired his release."

Soto's smile was brittle, nervous. "Thank you, Ivan."

He gave her a nod.

She hesitated before leaving. "I almost forgot." She turned back to him.

Perhaps now he would have an answer to this nagging doubt.

"Tallant, her associate, mentioned that another investigator from his agency is coming here. Aboard a private jet, I believe."

"Interesting." Romero would see to that matter. "If you recall anything else, you'll let me know."

"Of course."

He watched as she hurried down the cobblestone drive to her car.

Strange, he considered as she circled the fountain and drove away. She'd parked on the far side of the magnificent fountain he'd had imported from Spain. Generally she drove right up to the front steps.

That heavy feeling revisited him.

To the man who had attended to Vandiver's transport accommodations, Romero said, "Watch her. See that she makes no misstep."

Romero considered Soto's taillights as they faded into the darkness. The past twenty-four hours had been quite peculiar.

"She's secured," Lott informed Romero as he approached the door where Romero still stood.

"Excellent." Romero closed the door and inhaled a deep, satisfying breath. "I have a few preparations." His gaze settled on that of his most trusted employee. "Then I'll be ready to proceed. Her associate is expecting support to arrive via a private jet. Take care of that for me, please."

"Yes, sir."

Romero surveyed the luxurious foyer that greeted his visitors. Two decades of hard work had gone into his life here in Vegas. This was his world—his empire. Nothing transpired within his domain without his knowledge and his approval. Maintaining power had not been easy. Others came and went in hopes of tipping the balance, but each one proved unsuccessful. For one reason and one reason only. Romero understood the importance of patience and timing.

His watcher in Chicago had informed him of Nora's departure and intended destination. By the time she'd gotten settled into the Palomino, Romero had already prepared for a move. Still, he'd waited for the right opportunity. Timing was everything, after all.

For five years he'd had various sources keeping watch on Nora. Recording her comings and goings. Keeping tabs on who she called and why. Not once in all that time had she contacted his wife, as he had hoped she would. Not once.

Five years was long enough to grieve. The grief had eventually given way to bitterness.

Now he was simply determined to have his rightful vengeance. He could not locate his wife and child. His eyes closed as he dared to wonder whether the child had been a boy or a girl.

His child.

One Nora Friedman had denied him the privilege of loving.

Now she would know the agony…the endless torture he had endured.

His first inclination had been to watch her die for daring to steal from him.

But then he'd decided upon a much more fitting punishment.

She would live.

As he climbed the sweeping staircase to the second floor, his mood lightened. Today would be a thrilling victory. The plan was a brilliant masterpiece. It was, in part, his reasoning for waiting until the lovely Nora was back within his dominion.

Oh, yes. This day was well worth the wait.

He paused at the first door to the right of the spacious landing and rapped twice.

The door opened and his personal physician peered at him over his bifocals. "You're ready?" he asked.

Romero patted his shoulder. "Not just yet, but within the hour we will proceed."

His old friend nodded. "I'm ready. The patient has been prepared?"

The look that passed between them fueled Romero's anticipation. His old friend had anticipated this opportunity very nearly as much as Romero himself.

"Lott is taking care of that now."

Romero moved on to his suite. All was in place. As soon as he had news of the P.I.'s movements, they would begin. In his suite he crossed to the monitor and selected the underground-level surveillance.

Lott had opened the door to the cell. Nora, dressed now, faced him fearlessly. Romero had liked that about her. She showed no fear of anything. Few women possessed such a courageous nature. He wondered if that would change after today.

"Turn around and face the wall," Lott ordered the prisoner. "Put your hands flat against the wall."

In true Nora fashion, she rolled her eyes,

then did as she was told. She had little other choice. Lott entered the cell with his weapon palmed this time.

Nora made a sarcastic comment, but Lott ignored her. He removed the hypodermic needle from his jacket pocket while she rambled on about kicking his butt again the next opportunity that arose.

Lott stabbed the needle into her right shoulder. She stiffened, tried to twist away, but it was too late.

The muscle relaxer was in her bloodstream now. Within the next half hour she would feel the effects, slowly but surely leaving her defenseless.

And ready for payback.

Chapter Eleven

4:03 a.m.

Ted held his position in the copse of trees and shrubbery bordering the rear patio and pool area.

The house's exterior was lit up like a runway. The landscape lighting alone prevented any hope of moving closer to the rear of the house without being spotted by anyone monitoring the property. Every light in the house appeared to be glowing. Leaving him trapped in the small island of foliage.

Luck had been on his side in the beginning. Soto had parked near the massive water fountain, between it and the iron gates protecting the driveway from unauthorized entrance. She had explained that no guard was posted at the gate. Surveillance and access were controlled from inside the house. She had felt confident that surveillance would be focused on her as she emerged from her car and walked to the front entrance, giving Ted an opportunity to make a move.

Even before she had gotten out of the car, something unexpected had gone down inside the house. Security personnel had flooded the yard, front and back, surrounding the house. Soto had frozen, certain that Romero had somehow recognized she was not in the car alone. Ted had persuaded her to remain calm from his position hunkered down on the rear floorboard.

Finally, she had comprehended that whatever was happening wasn't about her and had given Ted an all-clear sign as the search appeared to move fully to the rear of the house. She'd gotten out of the car and moved toward the front entrance. Ted had slipped out of the car and disappeared into the landscaping.

Thankfully most of the exterior lighting in the front of the house was focused on the fountain, leaving an avenue of cover within the shadows. Soto had given him the layout of the property, including as much knowledge as she possessed regarding the underground tunnels. One entrance inside the house. Romero had an elevator in his bedroom suite that stopped on the first floor for access, then lowered directly to the tunnel underground.

Another entrance was near the pool. That access was used by certain guests who had the distinct honor of being invited for a round of private gaming in the massive underground entertainment room that had made Romero a favorite among the Vegas celebrity visitors.

Ultimately the purpose of the tunnels was to provide an avenue of escape for Romero. A direct route away from the property to emergency transportation. The entertainment feature merely served as a cover.

A private physician also served on Romero's staff. According to Soto, he trusted no one else with his health care. Evidently the man had made numerous enemies.

Friedman sure knew how to pick them when she was making enemies herself.

Ted banished the thought. She was in serious trouble here. Lethal trouble. He had to find a way to get her out. Waiting on backup was out of the question. The contact Simon had arranged had provided Ted with the necessities to make a move. He wasn't waiting. She could be dead by then. According to what Soto had admitted, Romero had been waiting for an opportunity to enact his revenge for Nora's past involvement with him.

Braced to move, Ted watched as the last lingering member of Romero's security team moved inside once more. Ted's worry now was the possibility of electronic surveillance. Soto knew Romero had an elaborate setup but she wasn't privy to the specifics.

Once Ted made his move, he had to move quickly. No hesitation. No miscalculations.

Getting in wouldn't be a problem.

Getting out would be the challenge.

He made the move from the copse of lush foliage to the equally mature and thick shrubbery closest to the side of the house—mansion—where Soto had assured him the exterior entrance to the tunnel would be found.

Ted held his breath. Listened. Nothing other than the night sounds and the low hum of the outdoor lighting. The three sets of French doors leading into the back of the mansion's first floor remained clear.

Go!

Ted eased along the perimeter of the landscaping bed until he had no choice but to break away and head for the wide tunnel entrance with its open iron gates.

Down the steps.

Halfway down he spotted a small over-head camera.

Damn.

Don't slow down.

No hesitation.

Pulse thumping in his ears, he kept going.

He passed the first turn to the right. That one led to the private gaming room and to the house entrance. Soto had instructed him to continue forward. Two more turns. The first was to a corridor that dead-ended and the second continued to the emergency transportation setup.

The dead end was his destination. Soto had no idea what was along that corridor since no one was allowed to that point. But she'd gotten the impression that anyone who crossed Romero ended up there. She knew for certain that the final turn led to the helipad because she'd had a short-term relationship with a member of Romero's security team when she'd first moved to Vegas. She'd overheard a conversation between him and his boss, Quinton Lott. Not once had she ever breathed that information, for fear of ending up scavenger bait in the desert. But she loved Vandiver and was willing to take the risk now.

Ted hesitated. Two steel doors lined the corridor but nothing else.

The first door was open.

He eased closer to door number one, his weapon palmed and ready.

Empty.

Ted took a breath and moved silently toward door number two. Unlike number one, the door wasn't standing fully open, but it wasn't completely closed, either.

He held his breath. Listened.

"Go ahead. Kill me. You still won't have your wife back."

Ted froze.

Friedman.

She laughed loudly. "Or your kid."

"You'll soon know just how that feels."

Romero.

Adrenaline blasted Ted's muscles. Would Romero be in there without a bodyguard?

Not likely.

"Proceed."

Tension tightened in Ted's muscles. Was that an order Romero had just issued?

"She isn't properly prepared for surgery."

Male voice. Not Romero.

What the hell? Surgery?

"She's prepared enough," Romero commanded. "Place the gag in her mouth and get started."

The sounds that followed were mostly of Friedman ranting at someone not to touch her.

Ted leveled his weapon and kicked the door inward. "Don't move," he ordered.

The man he recognized as Romero stared at him in abject surprise.

Ted moved quickly into the cell, getting his back to a wall to prevent anyone from coming up behind him. "Release her," he commanded the man dressed in scrubs and attempting to put the gag in place. The doctor, Ted presumed.

Keeping the larger part of his attention

on Romero, who made no move to rush Ted, he couldn't restrain the astonishment washing over him at the idea of what the other guy, the doctor, appeared about to do.

What kind of maniac tortured his enemy with surgery?

Ted didn't even want to go there.

"My security team is on the way down," Romero said with utter calm. "Put your weapon down and perhaps I'll allow you to live."

"I don't think so," Ted argued. He pushed off the wall, careful to keep a bead right between Romero's eyes. "Maybe I'll let you live if you cooperate." Ted wrapped one arm around his throat and burrowed the muzzle of his weapon into the bastard's temple. "Now, tell your man to release her."

God in Heaven. Friedman was strapped to a gurney. A stainless-steel tray lined with surgical instruments and a portable overhead light, as well as numerous other gadgets one would see in a hospital O.R., surrounded the gurney.

This was like some sci-fi movie setting.

"Continue," Romero said. "He's not going to kill me."

As if to reiterate his words, the sound of running footfalls echoed in the corridor.

Time to take a risk.

Ted rushed the gurney, Romero in tow. He dared to shift the weapon's aim from Romero to the man in the scrubs. "Let her loose. Now!"

The man—doctor, whatever the hell he was—quickly loosened the straps holding Friedman down. Romero struggled against Ted's hold, shouting for his associate to cease. The doctor loosened the last strap, raised his hands in surrender and started backing away.

"Fool!" Romero roared.

"On the floor," Ted said to the man in scrubs, who immediately scrambled to obey. Then he stabbed the muzzle back into Romero's temple. Just in time for two security jerks to rush into the room.

"Kill him!" Romero squeaked out around Ted's choke hold.

"You even breathe," Ted growled, "and he's dead." Two beads had settled on him but Ted held his ground. He might just die today but Romero was going with him. "Hurry up!" he shouted to Friedman, without taking his attention off the two armed men.

Friedman scrambled off the gurney.

"Get behind me," Ted told her.

She bumped into his back as she got into place behind him. "Sorry," she muttered.

What was wrong with her?

"What's it gonna be, gentlemen?" Ted asked the two staring him down. "You can join the guy on the floor or you can shoot me after I splatter your boss's brains all over his nice suit. Up to you."

Romero tried to speak but Ted clamped down harder on his throat. The bastard clawed and pulled at Ted's arm, frantic squeaks accompanying his desperate movements.

"Now!" Ted commanded, ramming the muzzle deeper into Romero's skull.

Whether it was uncertainty or Romero's high-pitched squeals, the two held up their hands.

"Put your weapons down on the floor," Ted instructed, "and kick them this way."

The first weapon settled on the floor, then slid in Ted's direction.

"Facedown on the floor now," he urged as the second weapon scooted his way.

Friedman snagged one of the weapons and stuck it into Ted's waistband at the small of his back. Then she reached for the other one, almost falling on her face as she bent down. What was wrong with her?

"Let's go," Ted urged. There was no time to analyze her actions.

Friedman was out the door first, then shouted, "Clear!" over her shoulder.

When Ted had dragged Romero into the corridor, Friedman closed and locked the door, leaving the three men stuck inside until help arrived.

"The best way out of here?" Ted asked her.

She started forward, her movements somehow uncoordinated and sluggish.

He wanted to ask what they had done to her or given her, but there was no time.

Romero fought him every step, but Ted kept dragging him forward. It wasn't that difficult. Friedman was moving damned slow.

Ted was no fool. The two guards he'd locked in that cell were likely only a small portion of Romero's security team. There would be others…watching their every move.

What felt like two miles later they reached another steel door. She tried to open it, shook herself and then reached back toward Romero. She grabbed him by the wrist; he resisted. Then Ted realized what she was doing. He moved in closer to what was a scanner of some sort. Friedman pressed Romero's palm against it and the door opened.

More steps waited on the other side.

Friedman closed the door, set the lock. "They won't be able to get through." She blinked, then gave her head a little shake. "But they'll have others on the ground headed this way."

Which meant they still didn't have much time.

Friedman stumbled twice on the way up the seemingly endless stairs.

She'd assuredly had some kind of drug.

They went through the same routine at the next door. It opened into an enormous garage-style hangar. A helicopter and a military-style SUV waited beneath a collage of overhead fluorescent lights.

"This area is monitored, as well?" Ted asked her.

She nodded, pointed to four overhead cameras.

The first shot echoed in the space as

he took out one camera. Then two, three and four.

"Helicopter takes an access code to navigate the pad out the overhead door," she said as she swayed, then recaptured her balance. "And a key." She pointed a ferocious glare at Romero. "We need both."

Romero managed a rusty laugh. "Go to hell."

"What about the SUV?" Ted suggested.

"They'd find us in nothing flat with the helicopter."

"What if we disable the helicopter?" Ted offered, determined to make this escape happen before the rest of Romero's team got here.

"Tracking system," she said. "All Romero's vehicles have them. They'd find us almost as fast that way."

"Then I guess we have no choice but to head out on foot." He nodded toward the walk-through door at the end of the building, opposite the oversize garage door.

More of that hoarse laughter from Romero.

Ted had had enough of him. He adjusted his hold, applying the pressure just so until the bastard stopped squirming. When he was fully unconscious, Ted allowed his limp body to drop to the floor.

"You should've killed him," Friedman said, her speech slurred.

Ted started to remind her that they were the good guys, but she promptly spun toward the door. The gun she'd been clasping clattered across the floor and then she dropped like a rock.

He rushed to her side, checked her pulse. Strong. Respiration steady. He lifted her arm and let it drop against her side. Limp as the proverbial dishrag.

She was out.

Not much time.

Ted glanced at the SUV.

She'd said there would be a tracking device.

A quick check on Romero assured he was still out.

Only one thing to do.

Ted fired off a few more rounds, putting out the overhead lighting. He double-timed it over to the walk-through door and shoved it open. He listened for sounds of arriving company. Nothing yet. Retracing his steps with the same swiftness, he reached down and hauled Friedman up onto his shoulder, snatched up the weapon she'd dropped. He straightened and surveyed the interior of the large building. Two doors. One to a room with windows across the front. Likely an office. One with no windows. Supply closet? Maintenance shop? Weapon storeroom?

He turned to get a look at the other side of the building. Shelves lined with supplies. And another door. He moved toward that one since it was closest.

Locked.

Damn it.

He hustled over to the door next to the office. It opened with one twist of the knob.

A smile slid across his lips.

Bathroom.

That could work.

He stepped inside, careful not to whop Friedman's head on the door frame. Two stalls, urinal and two sinks. And another door. He didn't have high hopes when he reached for the knob with its keyed lock. Surprisingly it was unlocked. Supply and cleaning closet.

Quickly, he cleared an area on the floor in the closet and lowered Friedman there. Then he closed the door leading from the hangar into the bathroom. Moving carefully, since it was as dark as a cave now, he settled in the closet with Friedman and closed the door.

Though this would prevent him from seeing the movements of anyone who arrived or hearing any conversations, it was the safest bet. They wouldn't have gotten a mile on foot.

All he had to do was keep Friedman quiet if she roused.

Not wanting to be less than fully prepared, he went down on one knee, keeping his weapon palmed. If anyone came through that door, they were going to get a chest full of lead.

He pulled out his cell phone to give Simon Ruhl an update and to check on backup from the local police since Trinity Barrett wouldn't have arrived as of yet.

No service.

Damn it.

He'd have to wait it out.

Regularly checking Friedman's pulse and respiration, he attempted to relax to the degree possible.

The screech of the overhead door rising warned that they had company.

He swallowed back the doubt and focused on listening for an approach.

Shouts and the thud of boots on concrete reverberated through the walls.

It sounded as if an entire army had descended upon the garage-style hangar.

His pulse reacted to the nearness of danger. With Friedman in the condition she was in, he'd already done all he could do to protect her.

He tamped down the worry to clear his focus.

The walls shook with the slam of a door. As best he could determine, the office door.

They were searching the building.

The bathroom door opened with an audible groan. Ted stilled. The door banged against the wall. He held his breath.

Light seeped beneath the closet door. Disabling the bathroom light would have garnered suspicion.

Stall doors slammed into sidewalls, first one, then the other.

His mind abruptly jolting into gear, Ted reached up and turned the toggle that locked from the inside the door that stood between them and whoever was searching the bathroom. He unclenched his fingers just in time for the knob to turn.

Sweat beaded on his forehead as the knob twisted a second time. Though it was too dark to see, he could hear the metal-on-metal slide of the turning knob and then the wood-against-wood pressure against the door.

"Clear!" followed by the fading clump of footfalls allowed him to breathe again.

The last Romero had heard before Ted rendered him unconscious was that they would head out on foot. If they were lucky, Romero would order his men to initiate a search of the surrounding area.

That would buy Ted some time.

He strained to listen.

A swoosh and a bang accompanied the bathroom door flying open once more.

Ted tightened his grip on his weapon, prepared for battle.

The next sound sent some amount of relief searing through his veins.

Someone had needed to relieve himself.

"Hurry up, Elliott!" a male voice shouted. "We're heading out! They can't have gotten far."

The swift drag of a zipper, then, "Yeah, yeah, I'm coming."

Friedman moved.

Ted groped for her mouth, flattened his hand there.

She stiffened.

He leaned his face close to her ear and whispered, "Shh."

Dead silence echoed for one, two, then three seconds.

The toilet flushed.

The shuffling of boots across the concrete signaled the man's exit.

Ted squeezed his eyes shut and thanked God for small miracles.

She was moving again.

He put his face close to hers. "Don't make a sound. They're out there."

She went immobile.

Ted resumed his vigil, listening intently.

All they had to do now was remain perfectly quiet.

And wait until the building was clear.

Chapter Twelve

"Barrett just checked in."

Victoria Colby-Camp looked up from the report she and her son, Jim, had been reviewing. "And?"

Simon's grim expression warned that the news was not good. "He's been detained."

"Detained?" Jim Colby countered. "By whom? For what reason?"

Tension tightened in Victoria's chest. Her son had asked the questions knowing full well the answer. Ivan Romero. They had learned, as had Simon, in the last two hours that Romero manipulated law enforcement in and around Vegas. Simon's contact with the Bureau had warned that Romero was not only extremely dangerous but also ruthlessly vindictive. Having a private aircraft detained would be child's play to a man like Romero.

"According to the detective in charge," Simon explained, "he received an anonymous tip regarding the abrupt, middle-of-the-night arrival of a private aircraft from Chicago. One that, according to the anonymous source, was part of a drug operation."

Meaning Romero had learned that backup for Ted and Nora was en route.

"Has Ted checked in?" Victoria asked, hoping against hope.

Simon shook his head. "Nothing."

"What about Soto and Vandiver?" Jim asked, concern mounting in his tone. "Are they still in Vegas or have they made a run for it?"

"According to my contact, they returned to the Palomino Hotel." Simon checked his cell phone. "The last text I received indicated that Soto's sedan remains in the personnel parking area. I called half an hour ago and spoke with Ms. Soto, and she assured me they were safe in one of the VIP suites."

"She believes they are in no danger of repercussions from Romero?" Victoria found that difficult to accept since Ted had used Camille Soto as a way onto Romero's property. A man as cunning as Romero surely had seen through the ruse…unless he had not learned of Ted's presence. That was perhaps too much to hope for under the circumstances.

"She insists that is the case," Simon confirmed. "The suite is one set aside for special guests. She claims no one, not even a member of her staff, is aware of her and Vandiver's presence there."

Jim shook his head. "Impossible considering the high-tech security system in place. She's not being totally up-front with us."

"I agree," Simon went on. "I've asked

my contact to get as close to the Romero property as possible. We have to assume that both Ted and Nora are still there."

Simon didn't have to say that his contact's hands were tied. Overstepping his bounds in any manner could set in motion serious recriminations. He'd already been a great deal of help despite the risks. With no authorization or compelling evidence—other than Simon's word—he had taken it upon himself to do what he could to be the Colby Agency's eyes and ears on the ground in Vegas.

"Is there anything your contact can do to speed up the process at the airfield for Barrett?"

Jim had an excellent point. If Barrett could get past this stall, his hands would not be tied as were those of Simon's contact.

"He's made a call, but there's no guarantee. Loyalty to Romero runs deep." Simon hesitated a moment. "Ian is running down any additional information regarding Nora that might prove useful."

"I provided a full dossier on all my Equalizers," Jim challenged.

The ensuing tension threatened to push the oxygen right out of the room.

"Everyone has a history," Victoria put in quickly to defuse the escalating pressure. "We all have skeletons in our closets. Events from the past that perhaps were thought to have remained in the past. When they come back to haunt us, it's always a surprise. I'm certain Nora had no idea that Romero still carried such a grudge."

The frustration etched along every line and angle of Simon's face was in direct contrast to the cold-stone stare emanating from Jim's. These moments were impossible to avoid but now was not the time to be distracted.

"Of course," Simon agreed, breaking the ice first. "Nora would never knowingly endanger Ted or herself. I'm simply suggesting we take the steps we can to head off any future incidents of this nature."

Jim said nothing.

Victoria nodded her agreement. "That's

an excellent suggestion, Simon. Every member of our staff is well experienced and has, undoubtedly, made enemies."

The merger of the Equalizers with the Colby Agency had been smooth for the most part, but the transition still had a ways to go. Victoria had complete confidence that all would be as it should soon.

Barring an unfortunate outcome with the Vandiver case. She couldn't help feeling genuine concern for her cousin, despite the fact that the situation wasn't quite as one-sided as she had represented. The continued infidelity of her husband was a painful hardship. Yet recent developments would indicate that things were somewhat different than Heather had painted them.

Time would tell.... All parties involved needed protection until that end.

"Von will put together a risk assessment of all cases and/or situations involving my people." Jim shot Simon one last daring look as he turned away. "It'll be on your desk in twenty-four hours."

Victoria watched her son leave the

office she hoped he would one day call his own. *My people.* Jim had worked hard to fit in…to give his mother what she had wanted since the day he was born—to be a part of this agency. This was difficult for him. More so than perhaps even she understood.

He was a proud man, a stubborn man. But he had earned every ounce of that pride and determination the hard way. A way no human should have to.

"I apologize, Victoria," Simon offered when the sound of the door slamming had stopped echoing in the otherwise silence. "It was not my intention to overstep my bounds or to elicit tension."

"Your suggestion was fitting given the current circumstances." She mulled over the idea a moment. "Why don't we put together a similar report on our entire investigative team?"

Confusion flared in his eyes. "We have a thorough evaluation on everyone already."

Victoria nodded. "We do. Let's pull the

evaluations together into one encompass-
ing report for Jim to review." Her son was
studying the files on investigations for the
past five years. He'd reviewed the dossiers
on all staff members. He was no doubt
aware of the agency's stringent employ-
ment guidelines. Still, if such an act would
smooth over this latest ripple, why not?

Simon gave her a nod of understanding.
"I'll have Mildred take care of it as soon
as she arrives this morning."

One step at a time. The merger would
come full circle one step at a time.

"Simon," Victoria said, slowing his departure, "one last question."

He turned to face her again. "Yes?"

"Our supplier in Vegas." The Colby
Agency had a supply or incidentals contact in every major city across the country.
In this day of airline security measures,
there was no way to transport the necessary equipment required for unforeseen
complications. "Is there anything he can
do to assist us in this precarious situation?
Any support whatsoever?"

"Unfortunately, he, too, is hesitant to step on Romero's toes."

Who was this man that he wielded such power? Victoria had known such men in the past...*Leberman*. The mere name had the power to send a chill through her heart. But, in her experience, a man like that amassed power over time—a great deal of time—and by arming himself with like allies.

Though Ivan Romero possessed great wealth, his dossier read like a bedtime story compared to that of a bastard like Leberman. How had he accomplished such loyalty in such a short, somewhat unremarkable period?

No matter, Nora had, it seemed, made herself a ruthless and significantly powerful enemy. Victoria hoped Ted could salvage the situation.

For now, it appeared the case could wait. Heather, Victoria's cousin, was safe under the watch of Leland Rockford. Her errant husband, Dr. Vandiver, had been released by Romero and was, to their knowledge, safe for the time being. Determining the source of his and Heather's domestic trials would keep until lives were no longer at stake.

Victoria dismissed the nagging instinct that all was not as it should be where her cousin was concerned. "Thank you, Simon. I'm certain Trinity will find a way to rendezvous with Ted and resolve this situation. Waiting may be our only option for now."

"I'm afraid that is our only recourse at the moment."

Even the Colby Agency was bested at times.

Victoria's door swung inward with Jim's abrupt return. "We have another complication."

Victoria bolstered herself for the news. "What now?" This case had taken more sudden twists and turns than any other she could readily recall.

"Heather Vandiver is missing."

That unsettling feeling that had been nagging Victoria since receiving the first troubling call from her cousin grew stronger now, spread through her limbs with icy intensity. "But her husband and his mistress are still at the hotel in Vegas."

"As far as we know," Simon qualified. "We haven't had a visual in almost two hours."

"Without access to a private jet," Victoria countered, "that's not time enough to have made such a move." Even then it would have been difficult for Brent Vandiver to have made the journey from Vegas to L.A.

"Rocky can't be certain this wasn't Heather's doing," Jim explained. "He's checked in on her every half hour since midnight. She appeared to be sleeping soundly. Twenty minutes ago he went to her door, felt something looked a little off and entered the room. As soon as he'd stepped past the open door, he was hit by a Taser. When he recovered, she was gone. There's evidence that the security strip on an exterior side door was tampered with. The door was left standing open. Heather's purse, keys, everything was still in the house. Only she was missing."

"But he isn't convinced that this is a true abduction," Victoria said, reading between the lines of her son's assessment.

"Not one hundred percent. The security system at the Vandiver home is top-notch. No one would have gotten past Rocky," Jim declared. "That I can guarantee one hundred percent."

"She could simply be worried about her husband," Simon offered with little enthusiasm. "The idea that he was in actual danger may have made her see things in a different light. Perhaps she decided it would be best if she sought him out without outside interference. Panic may have motivated her to set such a ruse in motion."

"Or," Victoria offered, "she could actually be missing. And in danger."

"Or," Jim countered once more, "intent on ensuring she has an alibi for carrying out her true plan."

Vandiver had claimed when he'd spoken to Nora that Heather was the one who wanted him dead, not the other way around.

"Either way," Jim recommended, "we need someone watching Vandiver and Soto every bit as much as we need someone providing backup to Nora and Tallant."

And their hands were tied.

There was no time to get another investigator on the scene. Local Vegas law enforcement couldn't be counted on where Romero was concerned.

"I'll touch base with my contacts once more," Simon offered, "but I wouldn't count on anything more than what we've gotten already."

"We need Trinity on Vandiver and Soto now."

Jim was right. Victoria banished the fear that wanted to harden like stone in her stomach. That would leave Ted and Nora on their own.

Against an enemy like Ivan Romero.

Las Vegas, 5:20 a.m.

THE WHOP-WHOP-WHOP OF the helicopter did nothing to soothe Romero's fury. For almost half an hour they had been sweeping the landscape with the spotlight. Back and forth, round and round.

Nothing.

Three SUVs combed the terrain, as well. Not a sign of Nora and her accomplice had been spotted.

Romero had checked in with the two guards who'd remained at the house and still nothing.

The two had to be hiding. Nora knew the area fairly well. But did she know it well enough to find her way in the dark under the circumstances?

The muscle relaxer had to be playing havoc with her ability to think and focus.

A new wave of fury tore through Romero's chest. He should have killed her when he had the chance. Should have killed her accomplice, as well.

Hell, he should have killed them all.

There was only one way Tallant had gotten onto Romero's estate.

Camille.

She would pay for her deceit.

So would her new lover.

No one crossed Ivan Romero and lived to tell about it.

Why had he ever allowed Nora to live this long? Why had he needed such an elaborate plan of revenge?

Because no one else had ever hurt him the way she had. He'd needed her payback to be special…to last longer than the few minutes required for life to drain from her dying body.

She and her brave partner couldn't possibly have gotten far. They had to be hiding amid the desolate terrain below.

What he needed was a larger and more ambitious search party.

He activated the mic attached to his headgear. "Call my dear friend Medlock," he instructed his head of security. "Let him know that we've chased intruders from my property. There are certain documents they may have obtained copies of. He'll know what to do."

Romero relaxed. The sheriff would respond to the call for help instantly and with full force.

There wasn't a secret in this entire county that Romero didn't know.... Many he possessed tangible evidence of. No one, *no one,* wanted those secrets revealed.

This time he wouldn't bother with his elaborate plan.

Nora would die.

And so would her friend.

Chapter Thirteen

5:25 a.m.

"I can carry you."

If Nora's eyes had responded to the command sent by her brain, they would have rolled. "I can walk. Get off my back. We don't have time for this." She'd told Tallant five times she could do this.

Even as she roared the argument, she swayed.

He steadied her. "I'm not so sure about that."

"Are we going to stand here and argue about this until they come back?" They needed to get out of here!

He didn't look happy but he put up his hands in defeat. "Okay. Let's do it."

Both the helicopter and the SUV were gone from the massive hangar. They'd heard the helicopter overhead as it tracked from north to south in a steady, relentless pattern. Romero wouldn't stop until he found them—that she knew for sure. Standing here, waiting around for him to realize they weren't out there anywhere, was not a brilliant idea.

With the helicopter sweeping its spotlight over the terrain, and the SUV and likely other vehicles combing the area by ground, it wouldn't take that long for Romero to come to that realization.

Their only option was to go back into the tunnel and take their chances back at the house. Romero would have most of his security force involved in the search with him. Minimal guards would remain at the house. One or two maybe.

She and Tallant were armed. Those were odds they could live with.

Tallant snagged her right hand in his left and moved toward the tunnel entrance.

Nora stumbled after him, her gaze glued to the way his big hand engulfed hers…the manner in which those long, strong fingers curled around hers.

He hesitated at the steps leading downward. "You're sure you can do this?"

Nora blinked back the pharmaceutical haze that still fogged her vision and glared at him. "Go!" She was fine. His grabbing her hand had distracted her, put her even more off balance…sort of.

As he dragged her forward, she reached around to the small of her back and pulled the weapon from her waistband. She wasn't a lefty, but she'd rather have the weapon in hand than not. Tallant had already palmed his and held it in a readied position. He was braced for confrontation. And confrontation was a given.

Focusing on each step was necessary. Her equilibrium wasn't back to normal by any means. Whatever they'd injected her with—a muscle relaxer of some kind, she believed—it hadn't fully worn off yet. The walls shifted a little, but only in her mind. Oddly, she was glad for Tallant's strong hold on her hand. He kept her moving forward. She was pretty sure that a couple of times she would have stopped otherwise, particularly on the descent of the steps.

Her throat and mouth felt sand dry. Her vision wasn't anywhere near up to par. And her balance was way off. But she was upright and moving forward. Tallant lugged her along behind him, his determined steps barely a whisper of sound and in sharp contrast to her drunken shuffle.

If they got out of here alive, it would be entirely his doing.

Tallant halted.

Nora bumped into his back. Though she'd realized he had stopped, her depth perception was suffering from the drug, as well.

Tallant held the barrel of his handgun to his lips, cautioning her to remain silent.

The branch of the tunnel that led to the two holding cells was up ahead. If a member of Romero's security team waited around that bend, there was no way for them to know until it was too late.

Struggling to keep her steps silent, Nora stayed close behind Tallant as he moved forward once more. When they were less than five yards from the door, he indicated for her to sit tight.

She didn't like it but she didn't argue. Frankly, she was in no condition to trust her judgment.

He eased closer and closer to the intersection of the two tunnels. Nora held her breath, braced to move into firing position.

Tallant checked the adjoining corridor, then sent her an all-clear sign.

Relief made her already wobbly knees a little weaker. She hurried after him, surprised at how quickly she could move now that it was safe to do so. Adrenaline probably. She needed more of it to neutralize the effects of the drug.

However, getting it by the usual methods—fear, anger, panic—wouldn't exactly be a good thing just now.

When he closed his hand around hers once more, a little shot of heat seared through her. She shouldn't have enjoyed it…but she did.

No sound up ahead or behind them. The coming fork would take them to the house. One route led to the pool and entertaining area, and the other to Romero's private entrance that led to his study on the first floor and on up to his bedroom suite on the second.

Nora tugged on Tallant's hand. He hesitated, stared down at her. She gestured to the left, which would take them to the pool and entertaining area. He nodded his understanding and started in that direction. Another of those small heat bursts accompanied the idea that he trusted her to make that decision.

Maybe he wasn't such a bad guy, after all.

That he'd risked his life to rescue her spoke volumes. The way she'd treated him, it was a miracle he'd bothered. Then again, she would have done the same for him—complaining the entire time, of course. And in the end either one of them would have been required to answer to Victoria Colby-Camp. That alone was motivation enough to do the right thing.

She hadn't really paid any genuine attention until now, but Tallant's shoulders were seriously wide. Blocked her view of anything else. His curly blond hair was boyish, yet there was nothing boyish about his muscular body. Or those intense gold eyes.

Apparently the lingering effect of the drugs was making mush of her brain.

The private gaming room was dark, the door closed. Only a few more yards now. Her pulse reacted to the potential for danger.

As they neared the top of the steps leading to the pool and entertaining area, Tallant hesitated once more. Nora listened, as did he. The trickling of the water fountain was the only sound.

But that didn't mean a guard wasn't standing just on the other side of the shrubbery shrouding this entrance. Again, Tallant signaled for her to stay put. Not arguing, she leaned against the wall while he rose to the landing and surveyed the area behind the house.

That he moved away from the landing and the meager cover of the shrubbery had her heart kicking into a more rapid rhythm.

She shifted her weapon to her right hand. Her palms were sweating, but her mouth and throat remained intensely dry. Cocking her head, she listened for noise beyond the water sound.

Seconds turned to a full minute. Had he run into trouble beyond her hearing range?

One step up. She was still several from the landing. It couldn't hurt to get a little closer.

One more.

Another.

Two steps from the top.

Deep breath.

She reached the landing and took stock of the situation.

The area was deserted. Ambient lighting sparkled against the water and highlighted the elegant plantings around the natural stone patio.

Where the hell was Tallant?

All sets of French doors along the back of the house remained closed, while the interior glowed like a shopping mall open for business.

But there wasn't a human to be seen.

Somewhere beyond the walled entertaining area a dog howled. Another excellent reason they hadn't tried that route for their escape. Her ankle burned with the memory of her close encounter with the K9 kind.

Okay. No Ted Tallant.

If he had been captured, she owed it to him to help despite her handicap at the moment.

Gripping her weapon with both hands, she moved toward the back of the house.

That soft trickle of water now sounded

like a raging waterfall roaring in her head.

Keep moving. Focus. Listen for any sound. Look for any movement.

Her head suddenly swam. She stalled, regained her equilibrium before taking another step.

Foliage moved next to the French doors leading into the kitchen.

Nora blinked, lost her breath.

Tallant motioned for her to get back.

The French doors opened.

"Stop right there!"

Damn.

One of Ivan's jerk patrolmen.

Since his weapon was aimed at her, she decided not to toss out the smart-aleck remark on the tip of her tongue. Instead, she held still, offered a caught-in-the-head-lights look of distress but didn't lower her weapon.

"Slow and easy now, honey," he said as he took another step in her direction. "Bend your knees and ease down until you can lay your weapon on the ground. Then slide it toward me."

Tallant moved.

Nora dove to the ground and rolled to the right.

A grunt echoed as the men tumbled to the ground in a heap. One weapon lay a few feet away from the struggle. Tallant's remained in his hand, but the guard was attempting to simultaneously keep it away from his body and to bang it loose from Tallant's grip.

Nora scrambled to her feet, staggered a step or two. When the muzzle of her weapon was flat against the enemy's skull, she ordered, "Put your arms flat against the ground."

Both men stopped moving, but the guard hesitated before obeying her command.

"Now," she snapped, pressing the business end of the gun deeper into his hard head.

His fingers unclenched, releasing Tallant, and with obvious reluctance he spread his arms out on the ground on either side of him.

Tallant got to his feet and picked up the other man's weapon. "Do you always ignore your partner's orders?" he demanded as he belted the extra weapon.

Nora didn't have to wonder who he was talking to. How long would he have waited for this dude to come outside if she hadn't appeared? She shot him a look. "Only when my partner leaves me hanging."

"Let's go." Tallant motioned for the man to get on his feet.

"There'll be at least one more around here somewhere," Nora related as she scanned the area around the pool. "Ivan never leaves less than two on duty."

"We'll check the front first before going inside," Tallant suggested. Only it didn't sound like a suggestion; it sounded like an order.

Which was precisely why Nora ignored him. She shoved the muzzle of her weapon into the guard's groin. "How many? And where are they?"

Nora didn't have to look to know Tallant would be rolling his eyes. It was a cliché move, but if it worked, who cared?

"I'm not afraid of you." The scumbag punctuated his haughty statement with a less than polite term directed at her character.

Tallant grabbed him in a choke hold and shoved his weapon into the soft underbelly of his throat. "Afraid of me, hotshot? Guys like you don't do well in prison, and I promise you, if either of us ends up dead, that's where you're going."

Just for the heck of it, Nora gave him a jab in the family jewels with her weapon.

"One more. He's out front," wheezed the guard.

Nora smiled. "See how easy it is to play nice?" She didn't wait to see what Tallant intended to do with the guy; she strode directly into the house.

WHAT THE HELL WAS SHE doing?

Ted disabled the guy, lowered him to

the ground and looked around for a way to secure him.

Nothing handy.

He removed the man's belt and fastened his hands behind his back. Wrenched off his shoes and used his socks to secure his ankles. That would hold him for a while. On second thought, he grabbed a towel from the neatly folded stack on the bar near the pool and shoved a portion of it in his mouth to keep him quiet when he regained consciousness. With another quick glance around, he opted to drag the guy into the shrubbery so he wouldn't be readily noticed if anyone came around to the back of the house.

Since he hadn't heard any gunshots or breaking objects, Ted had to assume that Nora hadn't encountered anyone inside.

Still, he went in silently.

The house was well lit. Quiet. No sign of Friedman.

The kitchen was clear.

He moved toward the wide entry hall.

Friedman waited, a finger pressed to her lips.

Ted surveyed the soaring two-story hall. No sound. Nobody.

She pointed to the door across the expanse of gleaming marble from where she stood.

He tapped his gun and sent her a questioning look. She shook her head no in response to his query as to whether there was another guard.

A voice beyond the towering front entry doors yanked their collective attention there.

The polished brass knob turned.

As if they had choreographed the move, both Ted and Friedman rushed the door, took a position on either side, careful not to make a sound.

When the door opened, Ted hesitated before ramming the muzzle of his weapon into the man's temple.

"Yes, sir. All clear here." The guard's hand dropped to his side, cell phone clutched in his palm.

Ted moved in. "Give me the cell phone."

Before the guy could react, Friedman had reached beneath his jacket and snatched his weapon.

"The phone," Ted demanded.

The guy reached out, dropped the cell in Ted's palm.

"On the floor," Ted ordered.

"They'll be back here any minute," the guy warned as he dropped down to his knees.

"And we'll be gone," Friedman taunted.

"Hands behind your back," Ted ordered.

Friedman, weapon leveled for confrontation, eased back toward the door she'd initially been watching.

Listening for any trouble she might encounter, Ted quickly secured the man on the floor the same as he had the one outside. He dragged him to the coat closet and shoved him inside, then grabbed a pair of gloves from the overhead shelf and gagged him.

Friedman was speaking, not the slightest bit softly, either.

Ted moved cautiously to the door she'd entered. A study or library. The gray-haired man who'd had Friedman strapped to that gurney stood in the middle of the room with his hands up. He'd exchanged the scrubs for an elegant suit. A cell phone lay on the floor between his feet.

"Check that phone and make sure he didn't put a call through," Friedman ordered.

Ted picked up the phone and checked the outgoing calls. "Not in the last two hours."

"Good." Friedman gave a satisfied nod. "I guess I don't have to kill you, Doc."

So he was a doctor.

"We should get out of here," Ted urged. "Romero could show up anytime."

"He will," the gray-haired man said, his head moving up and down with the same panic flashing in his eyes. "You don't want to be here if that happens." He looked directly at Friedman and said, "Trust me."

"We won't be here," Friedman assured him. "And neither will you."

Ted frowned at her. He had no intention of taking a hostage.

"He's our way out of here," she explained. "He knows the gate code. He's Romero's private physician." She glared at the old man. "And he knows what he gave me."

Ted could understand her reasoning. "Let's go."

Friedman pushed the doctor out the door, her gun jammed into his back. "I hope you have your keys, Doc."

The doctor nodded.

"Which pocket?" Ted demanded.

"Right jacket pocket."

Ted fished out the man's keys on the way out the door.

"That one." The doctor pointed to the luxury automobile parked to the right of the grand stairs leading up from the parking patio.

Ted disengaged the car's security system, careful to keep watch in all directions around them. There was only supposed to be two of Ivan's guards hanging around the house, but that could have been a lie.

Friedman ushered the doctor into the backseat, where she joined him.

Ted slid behind the wheel. When he'd started the engine and rolled up to the gates, the doc spouted the code. Hoping like hell he hadn't provided some kind of panic code, Ted entered the numbers and relaxed significantly when the gates swung open.

As soon as they were out the gates and moving at a nice speed along the highway, Ted pulled out his cell and checked for missed calls.

Five from Simon Ruhl.

As he put in a call to his superior, he asked Friedman, "Where're we going?"

"Back to the Palomino to find Soto." Friedman's gaze collided with his in the rearview mirror. "She had to have sold me out. I don't know how she knew—"

Ted launched into a conversation with Simon, cutting her off for the moment.

The news was not good, on any count.

This entire investigation had unraveled.

"Yes." Ted nodded. "I understand." He closed his cell and dropped it onto the seat. "We have several problems."

"You mean besides Ivan Romero and this old geezer?" Friedman bopped the doctor in the back of the head. "Just what the hell were you planning to do to me? And what kind of drug was I given?"

The doctor leaned slightly away from her, as if he feared she might whack him again. "A muscle relaxer. Only enough to relax you for…surgery. I would have given you an anesthetic for that."

"Surgery?" Friedman shouted. "Are you crazy? What surgery?"

"Since you deprived him of his only child," replied the doctor, his voice shaking with fear, "he ordered me to ensure you were never able to have any children."

God Almighty. Ted gave himself a mental shake to dislodge the idea of what would have happened had he not gotten to her before…

Friedman whacked the guy in the head again. "Idiot," she muttered. "Don't you know better than to work for a thug like that?"

"Nora."

She met Ted's gaze in the mirror. He'd known that calling her by her first name would get her attention. "I just spoke to Simon. Trinity Barrett is here, but he's been detained at the airfield. While we were incommunicado, Camille Soto and Dr. Vandiver apparently went underground. They're not answering calls and presumably are in hiding at the Palomino."

"That's where we're going," she said, fury rising in her voice. "I'm getting the truth out of that blond—"

"And Heather Vandiver has disappeared."

"What?"

Ted nodded. "She's gone."

"How the hell did she give Rocky the slip?"

"Taser. When he recovered, she was gone."

"She's on her way here," said Friedman, surmising.

Their gazes bumped once more in the mirror.

She didn't have to elaborate.

Dr. Brent Vandiver had insisted his wife had been trying to kill him. Maybe he'd been telling the truth.

Chapter Fourteen

"If you go in there, someone may recognize you," Tallant warned.

"You just take care of him." Nora tossed her head toward the doc in the backseat. "I'll take care of me." Just because she'd gotten ambushed once in the past twenty-four hours didn't mean she was incapable.

Tallant glanced at the rear window. They'd left Romero's pal in the car while they discussed the right way to enter the hotel and locate Vandiver and Soto.

"No offense, Friedman," Tallant countered, "but I'm not so sure you're up to the task. That drug may not have worn off fully yet."

Smart. He'd used the drug as an excuse rather than her lack of ability. "We don't have time to argue the point." Romero was likely back at the house by now. He would be livid and out for blood.

Specifically hers.

"Are you going to check every room?" he asked when she hesitated. "How long will that take? Chances are this will be the first place Romero checks when he finds we've given his security the slip."

All true.

Nora smiled. "Give me a minute." She opened the car door and scooted in next to the doctor. Why hadn't she thought of this before? "Camille Soto knows you, doesn't she?"

The doctor nodded. "Occasionally I attend to a guest here at the hotel. I do the same for others, as well."

The man was scared. That was good.

"If you called her and explained that

you needed to speak with her in person, does she trust you enough to give you her location?"

He shook his head. "She knows that my first allegiance is to Ivan...Mr. Romero."

Think! There had to be a way. Nora turned back to the old man. "What if you told her that Ivan had forced you to give Dr. Vandiver a slow-acting poison? If you don't give him the antidote immediately, it might be too late."

"That's ludicrous." He made a face that showed just how crazy he thought Nora to be.

"Ivan has done worse things," Nora said. She knew this for a fact. No doubt this man did, as well. He'd been planning surgery for her this very morning! "Things for which you are likely an accomplice." No need to point out the aforementioned scheduled surgery.

That seemed to get his attention. His demeanor shifted into defensive mode. "I don't know what you're accusing me of, but I can assure you—"

"Assure me of what?" she tossed back. "That you wouldn't have cut out my uterus if my friend here hadn't intervened?"

He blinked twice. "You can't prove that."

"Probably not," she admitted as she tapped her cheek with the cold steel muzzle of her handgun. "Any more than the police could prove I put a bullet in your head and dumped your body." She looked first at one side of the gun she held and then at the other. "This isn't even my weapon. It belongs to one of Ivan's men. The police wouldn't even investigate if they thought it would lead back to him. The two of you had a difference of opinion, and he needed you out of the way. Completely understandable."

Fear glittered in his eyes as he hesitated, likely searching for some way to save himself.

Nora shrugged. "Too bad for you." She started to climb out of the car.

"Wait."

She paused for him to gather his courage.

"I can show you where she is, but you have to let me go…unharmed once I've done so."

"Absolutely," Nora assured him without reservation and despite Tallant's questioning look. At the moment she didn't care why the doctor would have this knowledge; she only needed to find the lovebirds. If Vandiver's wife was indeed on the way here, she could be in danger or the other woman could be the target. Even Vandiver himself, for that matter. Nora and Tallant still had no clear evidence who was telling the truth in this fiasco.

If they could keep Romero off their backs, it was past time to clear up this mystery.

7:15 a.m.

"ARE YOU SURE ABOUT THIS, DOC?" Ted had taken the highway into the desert.

For the last ten miles or so there had been nothing but that desert.

"Yes. Another mile or so and there's a right turn."

Dawn had made its appearance, and now the sun was gearing up to bake the sand and towering mountains.

"Tell me, Doc," Friedman prompted, "why would you know about Soto's plan to come here? Your excuse that you treated a guest who'd stayed at this isolated retreat just doesn't cut it for me."

Ted glanced at the man via the rearview mirror. He looked nervous as hell. Whatever came out of his mouth, it wouldn't likely be the whole truth.

"She told me that she and Dr. Vandiver came here quite often to get away from the hotel…from prying eyes," the doctor said knowingly.

Possible, Ted decided. "Is this the turn?"

"Yes." The doc nodded with far too much enthusiasm.

Ted had a bad, bad feeling about this. "How far until we reach the place?"

"Only a couple of miles. It's the second of only three properties on this road."

Friedman studied the landscape. "I'm not familiar with this area."

She was suspicious, too. Ted heard it in her voice.

"It's private," the doctor explained.

"Does Ivan own this property?" asked Friedman.

Ted had considered that possibility.

"Yes," the doctor replied. "He purchased the properties for those who prefer some distance from the constancy of the Strip."

"Why would Soto come here?" Ted demanded. Time to get the real scoop. "Is she that close to Romero?"

"She owes him a great deal," the doctor confessed. "She rose to manager because of him. She's no fool. This is the last place he would look for her if he suspects she's double-crossed him."

Maybe so. One thing was certain,

Friedman had been right. Soto had likely sold her out. The question was, how would Soto have known who Friedman was?

"There!" The doctor pointed up ahead. "It's the next property."

Ted made the turn into the first property.

"What're you doing?" the man demanded. "This is the wrong place."

"And that's the one where Soto is, right?" Ted pointed to the small Southwestern-style house on the right a little farther down the sandy road.

The doctor nodded. "Yes…but…"

"Then we're good," Ted told him.

"Looks like no one's home," Friedman said aloud as they rolled up to the house across the road from the one Soto occupied.

Ted pulled the car around to the backyard and got out. While the doctor argued with Friedman, Ted checked out the place. Definitely no one home.

He circled the wraparound deck, paused at the front door long enough to take a good look at the place across the road. Soto's sedan was parked out front.

Then, because humans were creatures of habit, he reached down and checked beneath the welcome mat. No key. Then he reached up to check the molding across the top of the door.

A key.

He opened the door and went inside.

Smelled of disuse.

Large great-room-style space that combined the living room, dining room and the kitchen. Massive stone fireplace for those cold desert nights. Down a narrow hall were two bedrooms and a bathroom. No linens on the beds. No soap or shampoo in the tub. A partial roll of toilet paper sat atop the toilet tank.

Nope. There hadn't been anyone here in a while.

By the time he'd returned to the great room, Friedman and the doc had made their way inside.

"Anything?" Friedman asked.

Ted shook his head. "I need to get closer, to make sure they're both in there."

"And alive," Friedman suggested.

"And alive," Ted agreed.

"I don't understand," the doctor said. "I thought you intended to—"

"Secure him," Ted told Friedman. "I'll be back as soon as I've had a look."

"Come on, Doc." Friedman pushed the older man toward the narrow hall.

The doctor's incensed complaints followed Ted out the door.

He opened his cell to put through a call to Simon, but again, there was no service.

Damned desert.

There wasn't a lot to use for cover, but Ted utilized what was available. Rocks, sand, a few scrub bushes. Mostly he used a wide berth. If Soto and Vandiver were inside and worried about unexpected company, they would be keeping an eye on the road.

The closer he came to the neighboring house, the more care he took in his movements. He wasn't aware of Soto or Vandiver carrying a weapon, but there was a lot in this case that no one had been aware of.

In the rear a deck and basic landscaping foliage provided a small amount of cover. He chose what he hoped would be a bedroom window for taking his first look inside and eased closer.

No television or music sounds inside. No conversation, either.

He hoped the two hadn't been executed.

Drapes were drawn over the window with just enough of a crack betwcen them for him to get a narrow view inside. He studied the scene a moment to ensure he had a firm visual on both Vandiver and Soto.

Definitely.

The two were not only there. They were very much alive and in bed, expressing their mutual desire.

One window at a time, Ted checked them all. Like the house across the road, two bedrooms, a bath and a great room. No one else appeared to be in the house. The only sign of occupancy was the trail of clothing the two had made starting in the great room.

Somehow he had to figure out a way to get word to Simon that he'd found the missing lovers and there was no sign of the spurned wife.

If necessary, he would send Friedman back out to the main highway to make the call.

As he made his way back across the road, a number of questions crossed his mind. If Soto had no fear of repercussions from Romero, why hide out? And if she did, this was not exactly the best hiding place. Romero owned the place.

Lastly, at this point would one of them actually be afraid the wife was onto them?

Or after them?

And why the hell had Heather Vandiver Tasered a representative of the agency she'd hired to help her?

Had it been someone else? Someone who'd slipped in beneath Rocky's radar and abducted the woman?

Too many questions.

No answers.

Chapter Fifteen

"Something is way, way wrong with this whole scenario," Nora repeated as she paced the main room of the house. The effects of the drug had finally worn off, or maybe she'd worked them off. At least she felt like herself again.

Despite the fact that neither of them had eaten in hours. They were utterly exhausted and things just kept getting more complicated. This investigation stunk to high heaven. No doubt the good doctor tied up in the back bedroom thought, so as well.

"I agree." Tallant plowed his fingers through his hair.

Nora shouldn't have been so captivated

by the move but she was. She was tired. Closing her eyes, she gave herself a shake. She needed sleep. And food.

"Our first priority," he said, drawing her attention back to him, "should be contacting the agency. Right now we're operating in the dark, and no one can help us if they have no idea where we are and what we need."

He had no service on his cell. She had none on hers. He'd suggested she drive out to the main highway and try it from there. She supposed that was the only logical thing to do.

"Wait." She didn't realize she'd said the word aloud until he turned to face her. "The doctor's a local. His carrier may have service out here in the middle of nowhere."

That nice mouth of his tilted upward on one side. "You may be onto something, Friedman."

Tallant dashed out to the car and retrieved the doc's cell, as well as the one he'd taken from the guard. "The guard's has a pass code, but the doc's has full service," he said as he entered the necessary numbers.

About time they had an actual break.

She collapsed on the plaid sofa while he gave Simon Ruhl an update. It would have been nice if he'd chosen the speaker option so she could hear the other end of the conversation, but he hadn't.

After a few more questions and pauses, Tallant finally ended the call. He placed the doc's cell phone on the table and sat down next to her.

"Trinity will supposedly be released from detainment within the hour."

"He's coming here?" They could use some backup. Particularly if Romero's people showed up.

"Yes." Tallant propped his forearms on the knees of his spread thighs. "Unfortunately, that's where the good news ends."

"Great." They couldn't call the police. One guy—*one*—was on his way to provide backup. As soon as he was released at the airfield, that was. She and Tallant couldn't just leave, considering their job was to determine what the hell was going on with Vandiver and Soto and the missing wife. Speaking of which, she asked, "What about Heather?"

"The wife is still missing. There've been no hits on public transportation. If she left L.A. via public transit of her own free will, she didn't do it under her own name. We can't be certain she's headed here, but that seems the most logical move."

Which could possibly mean she hadn't done anything of her own free will.

Nora exhaled a big breath. "What're we going to do about Ivan?" He wouldn't give up. As long as they were within his reach, he represented a lethal threat. Yet they couldn't leave with this investigation unfinished. With more questions than they'd had before coming to Las Vegas.

Tallant stood, walked over to the dining table. "I've been thinking about that." He picked up the keys to the doctor's car. "I want you to drive out of here. Don't stop for anything but gas. Get back to Chicago as quickly as you can. Trinity will be here before long. I'll be fine until then."

Nora pushed to her feet. Didn't say a word until she got toe to toe with him. "Do you really believe I would ditch you? Just drive off into the sunset and leave you with this mess to clean up? Then you don't know me the way you think you do."

"Technically you would be driving away from the sunrise."

"Look." She stabbed him in that broad chest with her forefinger. "Just because you have a problem with me is no reason to play stupid."

He folded his hand over hers, capturing the offending finger in a strong grip. "This isn't about our bickering…before."

Somehow—maybe she truly had gone stupid—his eyes looked sad…worried. For her. She had to be imagining things. Yeah, he'd saved her butt back there. But she knew exactly where she stood with this guy—at the top of his frustration and irritation list.

"Then what is it about, Mr. I-have-to-prove-I'm-better?" This whole merger had been a bad idea. The Colby Agency investigators always had to come out on top, had to be right, had to be the heroes.

"It's about saving your life."

If he hadn't said it so softly, hadn't looked at her as if she were his top priority, maybe she wouldn't have had that deep ache tear through her chest. He couldn't possibly care what happened to her one way or another.

"If I go back, you win."

He closed those unusual gold eyes for a moment, as if it hurt too much to look at her. "You win. That's the way we'll write it up. I don't care about that."

"Forget it." She pulled her hand free of his and folded her arms over her chest. "I'm not leaving you here to face this insanity alone." She shook her head. "Not happening."

"You didn't want to work with me in the first place," he offered. "This is your chance to cut your losses. No one will think less of you for doing the smart thing."

She stared at those nice lips of his, wanted to pretend that she wasn't desperate to see what they tasted like. "Maybe I will." She lifted one eyebrow in challenge. "What do you say to that, Mr. Tallant?"

"That it would be the right decision. The smart decision."

"You really are crazy." She shook her head, told herself not to do what her entire body was urging her to do. "Fine...I'll..." She snatched the keys from his hand. "I'll just go."

"Stay off the beaten path," he advised.

He was willing to let her go—to let her run to safety while he stayed here and played the decoy.

She shoved the keys into his pocket. "No way. I'm not going anywhere."

He said nothing, just stared at her lips as if he didn't understand the words she had uttered.

"Stop."

His gaze lifted to hers. He blinked. "What?"

"Stop staring at my mouth."

He swallowed visibly. "I…was thinking."

Yeah, so was she. Usually that was a good thing, but in this case it was a problem.

He said nothing.

She said nothing.

They just stood there staring at each other.

"This is ridiculous." She grabbed him by the shoulders, went up on tiptoe and kissed him firmly on the mouth.

When she eased back down onto the soles of her feet, he just kept staring at her.

Maybe she should have left.

His arms suddenly went around her waist, pulled her against him, and he kissed her hard…long…deep.

The kiss was worth every moment of frustration and irritation and waiting.

His mouth was hot and firm and damned skilled. He tasted as good as he looked. Her arms found their way around his neck.

Her fingers threaded into his hair. She'd wanted to do that for so long.

He lifted her against him. Her legs instinctively wrapped around his waist as he turned and lowered her on the table.

She was already unbuttoning his shirt. She needed to touch his skin. The fire he'd ignited raged through her. Made her want to rip off every thread he wore. But just touching his chest...smoothing her palms over that rippled terrain was enough...for now.

Using both hands, he slipped off her shoes, then reached for the zipper of her slacks. She wiggled, the need swelling so fast, she could scarcely control her body's determination to meld with his.

He dragged the slacks down her legs, off one foot and then the other. He hesitated, stared at her injured ankle. "What happened?"

"It's nothing." She didn't want to talk.... She wanted him to continue what he'd started. When he still hesitated, she muttered, "One of Ivan's dogs."

"We need to take care of that."

"Later." She moved his hand up her thigh. His fingers splayed on her skin, made her gasp.

He burrowed two fingers beneath the silk of her panties.

She bit down on her lip to hold back a cry of sheer want.

For one long moment he hesitated again. When her eyes fluttered open, she realized that he was staring out the window, checking the house across the road.

A smile tugged at her lips. He wanted her. No doubt about that. She could feel how hard he was. But he wasn't about to fall down on the job. She liked that a lot. He was a man after her own heart.

Convinced there was no immediate threat, he wrenched open his trousers. She helped, sighing with satisfaction as her fingers wrapped around his full arousal.

He pushed the damp panel of her panties aside and thrust inside her. Her body contracted, drawing him more deeply inside.

He leaned down, braced an arm on the

table on either side of her, then kissed her. Softly at first. He held still when she desperately wanted him to move. To kiss her harder. To start that rhythmic friction her body was screaming for.

She loved the feel of his skin…the sensation of how completely he filled her. And the taste of his lips. She'd told herself she wanted to slap his face so many times. But it wasn't true. She'd wanted to kiss him. To shut that smart mouth of his by covering it with her own. To have him just like this…someplace wholly inappropriate and dangerous.

The waves of completion started deep inside her. She bucked to get him moving. She couldn't wait any longer. She needed him to…to keep touching her. His hands began to slowly trace her body. Rubbing, squeezing her breasts. Lifting her hips just enough to bury himself more completely inside her. Then those skilled fingers flowed over her bare legs, positioned them forward for deeper penetration.

She couldn't stop it. She came.

He held still and watched.

When she could think again, she grabbed him by the back of the neck and pulled his face to hers. She kissed him so hard, their teeth scraped together. She wrapped her legs around his waist and started a rhythm of her own. He growled into her mouth. She didn't slow, just kept pumping, dragging her hot, slick walls along that hard, solid length.

He tried to slow her frantic movements, but he couldn't control her.... She couldn't control herself. She was lost to the rhythm and to the new rise of pleasure.

He pulled her against his chest, carried her to the wall next to the window.

She was gasping for air as he took yet another seemingly endless moment to check out the house across the road.

How could he have that kind of discipline?

She couldn't think, much less see anything but *him*.

His gaze collided with hers once more and he gave her his full attention. He pressed her back against the wall and set his own ruthless pace. Her nails buried into his back. His mouth sealed over hers.

He drove into her over and over until she came yet again before he finally gave in to his own pleasure.

When his body was spent, he sagged against her, gasping for air just as she did.

"I wanted to do that," he murmured as he teased her lips with his teeth, "every time I watched you walk down the hallway at the agency. Every single time you lashed me with that wicked tongue of yours. I've wanted you so damned bad. I didn't want to…I called it a lot of other things. But *this* is what I wanted."

"I knew you'd be good," she confessed with a soft, breathy laugh. "I've watched you move." She rocked her pelvis into his. "Until I thought I'd go crazy if I didn't figure out a way to get you out of my system."

He searched her eyes. "Is that what we just did?"

She had to smile at his uncertainty. Usually it was the woman feeling uncertain about now. "No. I think you just planted yourself as deep as you can get."

He lowered his lips to hers, kissed her with infinite tenderness. How could a man capable of doing what he'd just done to her against the wall kiss so sweetly?

"I suppose," he said finally, when they both needed air, "we should get focused on the case again."

"Yeah." She rubbed his nose with her own. "We wouldn't want to get caught with our pants down." She squeezed his bare bottom with both hands. "Now, would we?"

He smiled. "Guess not."

She really, really liked the way he smiled.

She lowered her feet to the floor but hated so badly to let him pull away. That connection had felt more right than any she'd shared...ever.

Strange. He was the last person she'd expected to connect with.

Her abdomen clenched at the idea of what Ivan Romero had had planned for her.

If that vicious animal had his way, she would never know just how right things between her and Ted Tallant could be.

Chapter Sixteen

9:00 a.m.

Ted stood at the corner of the wraparound deck. Soto's sedan remained in front of the house across the road. That she'd parked in front felt wrong. Was it a signal?

There had been no traffic on this stretch of desolate road.

The only good news was that Trinity had been released after hours of detainment at the airfield. The problem now involved his getting here without being followed. Romero's people would be watching him. To come straight here would no doubt bring trouble right to their door.

None of that included the fact that Ted had stepped way out of line.

He'd made love to Nora...Friedman.

A knot of mixed emotions tangled in his gut. What the hell had he been thinking?

They couldn't stand the sight of each other. Working together had been the dead last thing either one of them had wanted to do.

But that had been before...before he'd known just how brave the sassy woman was. The risks she dared to solve a case.

And the way she'd stood up to a man like Romero.

She'd risked her life to save the life of another woman and her unborn child. Nora Friedman had sacrificed more than Ted could ever have imagined her capable to ensure the safe and happy future of a victim.

Incredible.

How could he have not known this about her?

Because he'd chosen not to look past the kick-butt facade she chose to wear. He now understood that, too. Self-preservation. She'd understood that she could never allow herself to be that vulnerable again.

He should have recognized the depth behind those exotic dark eyes.

He'd read the background on her. Born and raised in the L.A. area by a mother who kept a roof over their heads by selling herself on the street. An absentee father and no options for a future others took for granted.

Nora Friedman had raised herself, had made a life and a future without any foundation...without any help from anyone.

Ted hadn't given her an ounce of credit for that feat.

He'd been too busy fueling his frustration with her attitude.

He was a class-A jerk.

There was no other excuse.

"Look."

Ted turned to face the object of his disturbing musings. She'd managed to get within three feet of him and he hadn't even heard her approach.

Their situation was far too precarious to be so damned distracted.

"Everything okay?" He'd cleaned and bandaged her ankle with a first-aid kit he'd found in the doctor's car.

"Yes."

The way her arms were folded protectively over her chest and the somber expression on her face signaled otherwise. She was as lost in all this as he was.

She lifted one shoulder in a half shrug. "I wanted to dispel any misconceptions about what just happened."

Maybe it was her choice of words, but the idea that she would compartmentalize what they'd shared in such a way rubbed him the wrong way. Ticked him off, actually, and he didn't know what she intended to say yet.

"Let's hear it." He hadn't meant the words to come out in that harsh tone, but it was too late to take it back now. That she flinched tied some more of those knots in his gut.

"The last twenty-four hours have been

insane." She lifted one hand and made a vague motion of incredulity. "We've both been wired to the max, totally running on adrenaline."

Here it came.

"Sex is a natural survival instinct. We shouldn't feel awkward about it…or try to dissect it."

"I can't argue with that." Ted turned to scope out the place across the road. There was no reason to debate the point. She obviously didn't feel anything remotely related to a connection—other than the physical. And he…well, he didn't know how he felt.

Now wasn't the time to delve into personal affairs. He knew better.

"I'll check on the doc."

Ted didn't say anything to that or even spare her a glance. Time to get back on track. Without, as she had so eloquently put it, making more out of the moment than it was.

The thought left an emptiness inside him.

He pulled the doctor's cell phone from his pocket and checked the time. Trinity should contact him soon. Simon's Bureau contact hadn't seen any sign of Romero's people sniffing around the Palomino Hotel. By now he had likely given up the search for Ted and Nora. He would be checking flights, buses, rental car agencies. Eventually he would realize that the two of them were still here somewhere.

Romero would pull out all the stops then. He would shake out every sandpile and turn over every rock for fifty miles around Vegas until his gamble paid off.

And he'd found them.

The case—Heather Vandiver's case— kept them from making a move to protect themselves.

They were squarely between a rock and a hard place.

Definitely.

THE OLD GRAY-HAIRED GUY kept moaning and groaning until she removed his gag. "You need water?" She should have asked him that already. He wasn't really an evil person, just a greedy old bastard who'd gotten drawn into Romero's ugly games.

"There's no time."

"What're you talking about?" Nora didn't like the look of him. Paler than before. Feeble almost. "You need water."

"No." He shook his head, tried to wiggle his hands free of the bindings. "I tried to tell you before but you stuck that sock in my mouth." He made a face.

"It was your sock." No "six pairs for a few bucks" special, either. Silk socks. He shouldn't be so incensed.

"Please—" he searched her eyes with his own "—just listen to me."

She felt a little sorry for him, but not enough to untie him or get close enough for him to bite her or something. "Talk fast. I have things to do." Like wash the scent of Tallant off her skin. That her body trembled at the thought of his name made her want to scream.

She would kick herself for this later.

When she had Romero off her back and this case was settled.

"He'll come after us. It's a miracle he's not here already."

Now she recognized what it was that looked so different about the doc. He wasn't sick or feeble. He was scared to death. "What do you mean? He doesn't know where we are." Just because Romero owned the place didn't mean he would look here first.

"The car—" he swallowed with effort "—there's a tracking device on the car."

Adrenaline roared through Nora's veins. "Your car?" She knew this without asking.… Her mouth just hadn't caught up with her brain.

He nodded. "He'll kill me, too. You were supposed to let me go."

Holy… "Tallant!"

Nora raced to the front door, ignored the doctor's frantic shouts behind her.

Tallant stopped her bolt out the door with his wide shoulders. "What?"

"The car." She hitched a thumb toward

the back of the house. "It has a tracking device. Romero knows exactly where we are."

As if her words had summoned it, the military-style SUV, a trail of dust in its wake, barreled into view on the long sand and gravel road.

"Back in the house," Tallant ordered.

This was her fault. Other people were going to die because of what she'd done five years ago.

"I have to hide the doc." She didn't wait for Tallant's approval. When she reached the back bedroom, the old man had managed to get into an upright position on the bed and was ranting at her to help him. She shook him to get his attention. "Listen to me."

Miraculously his mouth closed.

"I'm going to untie you so you can hide." When he would have started his tirade again, she put a hand over his mouth. "Do what I say and you'll be fine. We'll tell Ivan that we tossed you out on the road without your cell phone or anything. Okay?"

He nodded. She dropped her hand away from his face and quickly untied his hands and feet. With a quick shove, she hid the bindings, including the gag, between the mattress and box springs. Then she considered the limited options for hiding the old man.

The doc was a smallish man. Not any taller than her and thin.

The one decent possibility that came to mind might just work.

"Come on." She grabbed him by the arm and headed to the great room.

Where the hell was Tallant?

In the kitchen, she opened the doors beneath the sink. The base cabinet would be a tight fit, but if he curled up and stayed put, it could work. She gestured inside. "Get in."

He started to argue but decided against it. The task wasn't easy, but he curled up and got himself jammed into the small space.

"Do not make a sound," she warned. "No matter what you hear."

He tried to nod but there wasn't enough room to do it right.

She closed the doors, palmed her weapon and moved to one of the windows that looked out across the front of the property.

The SUV pulled into the driveway and stopped midway between the road and the house. What were they waiting for?

Then she saw the first of Romero's team.

Another one...then another.

The three circled the house.

A fourth man remained at the SUV.

Romero was in there. Otherwise all four would have been surrounding or busting into the place, rather than only three.

Where was Tallant?

She moved noiselessly through the house to check out the views from other windows. Approaching each window carefully in the event one of those bastards had the same idea about getting a peek inside, she moved from one room to the next.

If Ted was...Tallant...if Tallant was

out there, the odds were stacked seriously against him.

Nora moved back to a window that offered a view of the SUV and its vigilant guard. Romero had to be in there. It was her he wanted. Getting Tallant killed was wrong. Just wrong.

If she provided a diversion, at least he'd have a shot at getting away.

It was her only option.

From her position to the right of the front door, she reached for the knob, gave it a twist, then swung it toward the opposite wall.

The continued silence surprised her. She'd expected the guard posted at the SUV to take a shot.

Keeping out of sight next to the door, she pulled the weapon from her waistband at the small of her back, checked to see that it was on safety, then tossed it out onto the deck.

Still no reaction from the guard.

"I'm coming out," she shouted.

No response. No sound at all.

Taking a deep breath, she sidestepped into the open doorway.

The guard leveled a bead on her, center chest.

The red spot from the laser beam confirmed her assessment.

Hands up, she started across the porch.

She felt fairly confident that he wouldn't shoot her. No, Romero wanted to savor that duty himself.

Down one step, then two.

Still no sign of Tallant or the other three from Romero's security team.

Strange.

But then, every damned thing about this investigation had been strange.

Third step. And then the final one to the ground.

She kept an eye on the guard as she approached him.

"Round up your friends and let's go," she suggested.

She didn't have to see his glare, couldn't since he wore sunglasses, but she could feel his contempt.

"Get in. Rear passenger seat."

"Whatever you say."

She walked around him to the passenger side and opened the back door.

"I'm really quite annoyed, Nora."

She smiled at Romero. "That—" she climbed into the seat next to him "—actually makes me happier than you know." She closed the door.

Before she could settle into the seat, the back of his hand slammed across her face.

Her cheek and nose stung, eyes watered. But she refused to make even a whimper of distress. She settled into position and stared at him. "You always did enjoy torturing those weaker than you." The whole getting knocked around thing was getting old.

"Only those who lack the discipline to follow my orders." He rapped on the window.

The guard posted at the front of the SUV immediately stalked to the driver's door.

Nora stole a glance at the house. Had

Tallant been taken down? If so, where were the three jerks who'd arrived with Romero?

"What's the status of the others?" Romero asked the man as he slid behind the steering wheel.

"Nonresponsive."

Hope bloomed in Nora's chest. Had Tallant managed to take down all three?

"Let's go," Romero ordered.

"We dumped your doctor," Nora said, more to distract him from the windows as the SUV backed toward the road than to give the doc a cover. "Hope you don't mind."

Romero shot her a glower. "My staff is fully expendable."

Nora wondered what his driver thought of that. "Where's your number one bully, Lott?" It struck her as odd that he hadn't arrived with Romero. Usually he would have been the one providing his personal security.

"He had an unfortunate accident," Romero replied.

The driver snickered.

Romero had killed him. Or had him killed. Nora's stomach clenched. For allowing her to escape.

"One day someone will stop you, Ivan," she warned. "It's only a matter of time."

He smiled at her. That repulsive, sinister expression that screamed of evil victory. "But not today." He reached into his jacket and withdrew a small-caliber handgun. Elegant pearl handle. "I've been saving this for a special occasion."

Nora's pulse skipped into a rapid staccato. "For blowing your brains out?" She couldn't think of anything more special than that.

That evil gaze narrowed.

"Oh, wait." She bopped the heel of her hand against her forehead. "What am I thinking? You have to have a brain before you can blow it out."

He jammed the shiny muzzle against her forehead. "You are not nearly so smart as you think, Nora. Your luck just ran out."

"What the hell?" echoed from the front seat.

The gun still boring into Nora's skull, Romero glanced at his driver. "What?"

"There's a car—"

Something hit the back of the SUV. Hard. Nora bumped the back of the seat in front of her. Romero did the same. The SUV sped up, propelling them both back into their seats.

Nora grabbed Romero's wrist, shoved his arm upward.

An explosion echoed inside the vehicle. Glass shattered behind her.

She shoved harder, pushing him into the door on his side of the vehicle. There was nothing she could do but try to keep the business end of the weapon pointed away from her.

Another jolt against the back of the vehicle, throwing Nora on top of Romero. His surprise gave her enough leverage to push his hand fully away from her.

A second explosion rent the air.

The SUV swerved…bumped across the ditch.

The weapon flew out of Romero's hand.

Nora scrambled onto the floorboard after it.

Romero climbed over the seat.

Nora's fingers wrapped around the pearl handle.

The SUV lurched.

A jolting stop.

Suddenly the vehicle was falling…onto its side.

Her stomach rocketed into her throat as she rolled with the momentum.

The crash seemed to echo forever.

For a moment she lay there, attempting to gather her wits. The engine still hummed.

Her fingers remained clasped around the butt of the weapon.

Where was Romero?

She got herself into an upright position and peered over the seat.

The driver's head was bleeding.

Romero lay crumpled between the steering wheel and the windshield.

Nora blinked. He was still breathing. No blood that she could see. His right leg was in bad shape. Twisted at an odd angle. When he regained consciousness, that was going to hurt like hell.

Only the driver was bleeding.

She reached around to check his pulse.

Shock radiated through her.

He was dead.

Then she saw the reason.

The blood had oozed from a small hole in the back of his head. She leaned down to get a look at his face. No exit wound that she could see.

Even though she didn't care if he was dead or alive, she checked Romero's pulse, as well. Just to be sure. She made a disparaging sound. You couldn't kill an evil bastard like that.

"Nora!"

Her heart leaped. Tallant…Ted. "Yeah, I'm okay!"

It took him a minute to get a door open,

but he managed. Tears welled in her eyes. If he hadn't given chase and rammed the SUV…

He pulled her out, dragged her into his arms.

"What the hell did you do that for? You should have stayed in the house."

She hugged him hard, the damned little gun still clutched in her hand. "I didn't want him to kill you because of me."

Ted drew back and stared into her eyes. "I had things under control."

She shook her head. Swiped at the moisture on her cheeks. "I didn't know. I was afraid…for you."

"Come on." He pulled her against him. "I called for emergency medical support. They'll be here soon. Trinity Barrett is on his way, as well."

She glanced back at the overturned SUV. "Maybe that bastard will die before they get here."

"He's not going to get away this time," Ted assured her. "The Colby Agency won't stop until he's finished."

That was one thing Nora understood now with complete certainty. The Colby Agency was a force to be reckoned with. Even if they did play so close to the rules.

She stalled. "There's another vehicle at the house where Dr. Vandiver and Camille Soto are hiding out."

Before the words were fully out of her mouth, Ted was running in that direction.

A little wobbly at first, Nora raced after him.

To Nora's knowledge, Mrs. Vandiver had not been found. The idea that Dr. Vandiver was convinced his wife was trying to kill him sent a new fire into Nora's muscles.

If she had given Rocky the slip…had gotten here somehow…

She might have killed Vandiver and his mistress already.

Chapter Seventeen

Ted pressed his ear to the wall near the front entrance in an attempt to make out the shouted words from inside.

Female. Two different voices.

Confirmed his assumption that Heather Vandiver was here. The rental in the driveway bore a California license plate.

He held up a hand as Nora neared the steps, then motioned for her to go around back. She hustled around the corner of the house.

Male voice.

Dr. Vandiver.

Whatever was happening inside, it was growing increasingly tense as Ted listened.

He reached toward the door, rapped hard.

The shouting stopped.

Ted banged on the door a second time.

Scrambling sounds inside had him reaching for the knob.

More shouts. A scream.

Weapon drawn, Ted burst through the door.

Heather Vandiver waved a handheld device at him.

Taser.

That certainly answered one question.

Dr. Vandiver stood next to the bed, his boxers hanging on his hips.

Camille Soto, the other woman in this awkward triangle, stood at the other end of the bed, a sheet draped around her.

"Who're you?" Heather demanded.

"He's from the Colby Agency," Soto said, her expression reflecting the terror in her voice. "He's here to protect Brent."

"Put down the Taser," Ted said firmly. "Put it down and we'll talk."

Heather shook her head, waved the

Taser. "No." She glanced at the gun but seemed unaffected by it.

"Dr. Vandiver, step away from the bed." Ted hitched his head toward the front of the house. "Move toward the door."

Vandiver sidled away from the bed.

"Don't you dare," Heather howled at him. "You're not going anywhere, you bastard."

Ted couldn't exactly shoot the woman. Her weapon wasn't exactly deadly—in most instances. In an effort to lessen the tension, he lowered his weapon. "Mrs. Vandiver, I understand you're upset. But this isn't the answer. Put down the Taser and let's call Victoria." He hoped the mention of her cousin's name would snap her out of this irrational state.

She turned her attention to Soto. "Do it."

Soto's eyes widened. "I...don't know what you mean."

Ted studied the woman wrapped in the sheet. She was lying. She looked scared as hell, but more than that, she looked as if she'd been cornered.

"I paid you," Heather shouted. "I paid you a lot of money."

Soto was shaking her head and inching away from the foot of the bed.

"You paid her for what?" Ted asked quietly. No need to amp up the anxiety level.

Heather jerked her attention toward him. "To kill that bastard." She nodded toward her husband. "He cheated on me one time too many. I wasn't about to give him a divorce and end up with only half of what I'd earned putting up with his indifference and infidelity all these years."

"She's crazy!" Soto shouted, stumbling back a couple more steps. "I don't know what she's talking about."

"That's impossible." Vandiver moved toward his wife. "You're lying."

Ted grabbed him by the arm and hauled him back. "Let's not get excited here. Look." Ted tucked his weapon into his waistband. "There's no need for this to get out of control."

Heather laughed. "I might be crazy, but at least I'm not stupid." She laughed again. "You thought she cared about you." Heather shook her head. "She was going to kill you." Her expression turned dark and angry. "But when she stopped returning my calls and the two of you disappeared, I knew I'd been double-crossed."

"Prove it," Soto challenged. "No one's going to believe you."

Heather nodded. "I thought you might say that." Heather reached into her pocket.

Ted's hand went back to the butt of his weapon.

Heather pulled a mini recorder from her pocket and waved it. "How's this for proof?" She pressed Play.

"I have a plan for taking care of him."

Camille Soto's voice.

"Make the deposit and this will be his last trip to Vegas."

A damning statement by Ms. Soto.

"I can't believe this," Vandiver muttered.

"You stupid, stupid man," Heather taunted her husband. "The only thing any woman would want from you is your bank account."

Sirens wailed in the distance.

"We'll let the authorities sort this out," Ted suggested, thankful help was close.

"I'm not taking the fall for this," Soto shouted. The sheet dropped to the floor, revealing her nude body and the handgun she'd been hiding under the wrinkled linens. "We'll just all go to hell together."

"Lower the weapon, Ms. Soto," Ted warned.

"You bitch!" Heather screamed. "You promised!"

"Since your antidepressants and sedatives didn't work," Soto said, leveling a bead on Heather, "maybe this will."

Ted dived at Heather, knocked her to the floor.

A bullet zinged past his ear, lodged in the wall next to the door.

"Get down!" Ted shouted at Vandiver.

Another gunshot.

Vandiver hit the floor.

Ted moved to scramble toward Heather.

A series of shots hit the ceiling.

Nora was struggling with the woman, the still discharging weapon's muzzle pointed upward.

Where the hell had Nora come from?

Ted grabbed the Taser and lunged into the fray.

He pushed Nora aside and jammed the Taser against Soto's naked torso.

She stiffened. The weapon clattered to the floor. Soto crumpled into a heap.

Ted turned to check on the others. Heather was crawling toward the weapon Soto had dropped.

Ted kicked the weapon out of her reach.

Nora jerked Heather to her feet and re-strained her.

Vandiver hadn't moved.

Ted knelt down next to him. The man

had covered his head with his arms. Blood spilled from his shin. He was hit, but it didn't look serious.

"Help is here, Dr. Vandiver," Ted assured him. "Let's get you out of the path of the door." He'd heard the slamming vehicle doors outside.

Vandiver shook his head, tears rolling down his cheeks. "I loved them both."

Ted glanced up at Nora, who still had a grip on Heather Vandiver. Nora rolled her eyes.

Ted stifled a laugh.

This wasn't funny.

It was crazy sad.

But, for this case, it was over.

Chapter Eighteen

Victoria closed the file on her cousin's case. She still felt some amount of astonishment at the news of her deadly deception.

Jim heaved a heavy breath. "I'm certain the psychological analysis will reveal the motive for this incredible turn of events."

Victoria nodded sadly. Jim was correct. Heather would be evaluated to determine if she was fit to stand trial. "I can't help feeling as if I should have kept in touch. Perhaps I would have noticed something was very wrong."

"Mother." Jim eased forward in his chair, braced his clasped hands on her desk.

It still made her smile when he called her "Mother." She should be accustomed to it by now, but perhaps she never would be.

"As much as you want to," Jim went on, "you cannot save the world."

"*We* can attempt to save our clients," she suggested, emphasizing the *we*.

He nodded. "One case at a time." He paused. "Simon's contact passed along the news that Ivan Romero is now facing a number of federal, as well as local, charges for his crimes. Camille Soto turned state's evidence against him to secure a lighter sentence for her part in the conspiracy against Dr. Vandiver."

"That's certainly good news." Victoria was immensely thankful that Nora had not become another of his victims. That monster deserved to spend the rest of his sadistic life behind bars.

"I've given Tallant and Nora a few days' R & R," Jim added.

"They made an excellent team." Victoria was quite impressed at how well yet another Equalizer–Colby investigator team had worked together.

Jim reclined in his chair, studied Victoria a moment. "*We* make an excellent team."

"Yes," she agreed. "We do."

"Tasha and I thought we'd host the annual agency barbecue at our house this year."

Tasha, Jim's wife, was a true jewel. Victoria couldn't be happier with her daughter-in-law. "That's an excellent idea."

The Fourth of July was coming up next week. Jim's suggestion was yet another step toward the complete cohesion of the merger.

"Perhaps Ian and Nicole will be able to attend," Victoria noted, "and show off the new baby." Ian Michaels was one of Victoria's seconds in command, along with Simon Ruhl. Ian and his wife, Nicole, had welcomed their third child only four days ago. Tasha, Jim's wife, was due any day

with their second child. Life at the Colby
Agency was truly blessed.

"Tasha would love that. She's so ready
for our son to be born."

A recent visit to the doctor's office had
confirmed that the baby was indeed a boy.
Victoria was beside herself with joy. Her
son couldn't possibly love his daughter,
Jamie, more, but she knew how very much
he wanted a boy.

"You and Tasha are still set on the name
you've chosen?" Victoria felt giddy each
time she thought of how thrilled her husband would be when he heard the news.

"Lucas James Colby," Jim confirmed.
"Luke."

Victoria's heart filled with pride. "Lucas
will be ecstatic."

The intercom on Victoria's desk buzzed.
She pushed the button for the speaker
option. "Yes, Mildred." Mildred, her long-
time personal assistant, wouldn't have in-
terrupted a meeting between Victoria and
Jim had it not been urgent.

"Victoria, Jim," said Mildred, sounding

a little giddy herself, "Tasha and Jamie have just left the Pier with one of Chicago PD's finest."

Victoria's breath hitched.

Jim sat up straight. "What happened?"

"Labor, dear boy," Mildred enthused. "The two of you need to get to the hospital now."

The next few seconds were a blur of grabbing keys and phones and shouting orders to Mildred as she followed them to the elevator.

Once they were in Jim's SUV and headed for the hospital, Victoria managed a deep breath. She turned to her son and smiled. "We are so very fortunate."

He braked for a traffic signal, sent a return smile in her direction. "Yes, we are."

She reached over and placed her hand atop the one he had resting on the console. "Finally." A realization struck Victoria. "Oh, my." She grabbed her purse. "I'd better call Lucas!"

Jim laughed. "He's former CIA, Mother.

He probably already knows and is at the hospital, waiting for us to catch up."

Victoria entered his number all the same. "You could be right."

She relaxed in her seat and waited for her husband to answer her call.

Together they would witness this miracle and welcome the newest member of the Colby family.

3:00 p.m.

NORA SHUT OFF THE VACUUM cleaner and listened.

Rapping on her front door confirmed that she'd heard something.

She hurried down the hall and to the door. A quick peek through the security peephole made her smile.

Ted.

He'd called her at midnight last night just to ensure she was okay.

How could she have ever thought he was anything less than sweet and…well, handsome as hell?

Truth was, she'd recognized the latter the first time she laid eyes on him. She just hadn't wanted to admit it.

She started to open the door but hesitated. With a quick glance in the mirror by the coatrack, she adjusted her wild ponytail. She looked a mess. Shorts. Cutoff tee. Barefoot.

This morning had brought a burst of energy. She'd gotten up in the mood to clean her apartment.

Not a normal inclination for her.

She blew into her hand to check her breath. Decided she was good to go. And opened the door.

"Hey."

He leaned against the door frame, the short-sleeved button-down shirt and faded jeans making him look even hotter than the suits he wore at the office.

"Hey, yourself," he said, the deep sound of his voice sending shivers along her skin.

"Come in." She backed up a step and opened the door wider.

"If I'm interrupting," he countered, hesitating to cross the threshold.

"Yeah, right." She gestured to the vacuum cleaner. "Like I wouldn't take any excuse to get away from that." Not exactly what she'd meant to say. "Come on." She grabbed him by the arm and dragged him inside.

"I didn't have you pegged as the domestic type."

Nora closed the door and turned to face him, hands on hips. "How exactly did you have me pegged?"

One corner of that sexy mouth tilted wickedly. "I'd better take the Fifth on that one."

"Would you like something to drink? A beer?" Was it too early to be offering beer? "Juice?" No man ever made her feel awkward. Somehow this one did.

"No, thanks."

"Then sit." She gestured to the sofa.

Thankfully she'd picked up before she'd started vacuuming. Her place had been a mess. Clothes and take-out boxes strewn all over the place.

He swaggered over to the sofa and settled on one end. She draped herself on the arm of the other end.

"So, what're you doing today?" They'd both been given rest days. Definitely a good thing, considering how exhausted she'd been when she finally climbed into her own bed last night.

"Went to the market. Picked up a few things." He shrugged those really nice shoulders. "Went for a run. Worked out at the gym."

God, she hated people who could work forty-eight hours straight and then still go to the gym. "I'm glad you had the energy."

"Habit."

She wasn't about to get on the subject of habits. Chocolate. Wine. Shopping. She had far too many habits in which she liked to indulge.

"I thought maybe you might like to have lunch."

That tingle that started each time she thought of him—even when he wasn't in the room—buzzed to life. "That could work." She stood. "But I need to change first."

"Actually—" he stood as well "—I meant *here*."

Her fridge was distinctly empty.

Before she could say as much, he added, "There's this great place just a few blocks from here that delivers."

"Chinese?" she asked, hoping he was thinking of her favorite take-out joint.

"Definitely. A sort of hole-in-the-wall, but the food is fantastic."

She reached for the phone on the table by the sofa. "I know their number by heart." She entered the number and made a mental note of what he wanted as she waited for an answer.

When the order had been placed and an assurance that it would be twenty to thirty minutes had been given, Nora dropped the phone back into its charger and rummaged around in her brain for what to say next. "Twenty to thirty minutes."

"Good. We can—" he shrugged "—talk for twenty to thirty minutes."

Her head was moving up and down in affirmation. "Talking is good."

"Get to know each other better," he said, clarifying.

"Yeah," she agreed. "There's a lot…to know, I suppose."

"I have two brothers," he said. "And my parents."

She nodded again. "No siblings. A mother somewhere in Cali." She probably should have explained that last part, but she couldn't stop watching his lips.

"I bought a house over in Hyde Park a couple of months ago."

"Nice." And his hands. He had the greatest hands. Broad, powerful…long, blunt-tipped fingers.

"I'm still trying to figure out the whole decorating and furnishing thing."

"Yeah, me, too." Her apartment, other than her meager furniture, looked exactly as it had the day she rented it three years ago. She wouldn't mention that, though.

"I guess we have about fifteen more minutes."

"Fifteen to twenty probably."

Not nearly enough time for what she would love to do with him.

Her heart bumped against her sternum when his gaze settled on her lips.

Their eyes met…and the polite conversation was over.

They lunged into each other's arms.

He kissed her. She loved the way he kissed. The way his hands moved over her body, lifted her against him.

"We don't have enough time," he murmured against her mouth.

"Fifteen minutes of foreplay." She nibbled on his chin. "We can save the main course for after the delivery."

He eased her back down on the sofa. "Sounds like a plan."

He cupped her breast, made a path down her throat with those amazing lips. She did not want to wait.

"Forget the foreplay." She reached for the fly of his jeans.

"I was hoping you'd say that," he whispered as he slipped his hands into her baggy shorts.

Ten seconds of stripping and he was inside her.

She closed her eyes, relished the incredible sensation.

She couldn't get enough of touching him...of having his weight against her.

It felt so good.

Just like the dream she'd had last night.

Hours and hours of making love with him.

She'd awakened with the strangest urge...the urge to make babies.

Maybe it was all the chatter about new babies at the agency.... Or maybe it was knowing how close she'd come to losing that precious capacity.

Whatever the case, Ted Tallant was definitely the man she wanted to make babies with.

As his lips melded with hers and his hips began that rhythmic pumping, she had one last fleeting thought.

She'd have to marry him first…make a decent man out of him.

Maybe she'd run that by him later…after this appetizer…and the main course…and maybe even dessert.

* * * * *

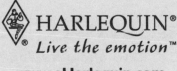

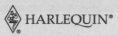

Invites *you* to experience lively, heartwarming all-American romances

Every month, we bring you four strong, sexy men, and four women who know what they want—and go all out to get it.

From small towns to big cities, experience a sense of adventure, romance and family spirit—the all-American way!

Love, Home & Happiness

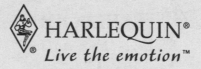

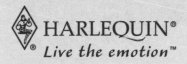

HARLEQUIN®
Presents

**The world's bestselling romance series...
The series that brings you your favorite authors,
month after month:**

Helen Bianchin...Emma Darcy
Lynne Graham...Penny Jordan
Miranda Lee...Sandra Marton
Anne Mather...Carole Mortimer
Melanie Milburne...Michelle Reid

and many more talented authors!

*Wealthy, powerful, gorgeous men...
Women who have feelings just like your own...
The stories you love, set in exotic, glamorous locations...*

HARLEQUIN®
Presents

Seduction and Passion Guaranteed!

HPDIR08

www.eHarlequin.com